The right of Sophia Lowell to be identified as the Author of
the Work has been asserted by her in accordance with the
Copyright, Designs and Patents Act 1988.

First published in paperback in Great Britain in 2010 by
HEADLINE PUBLISHING GROUP

5

Cataloguing in Publication Data is available from the British Library

ISBN 978 0 7553 7737 4

Typeset in ITC Stone Serif by
Palimpsest Book Production Limited, Falkirk, Stirlingshire

Printed and bound in Great Britain by
Clays Ltd St Ives plc

Headline's policy is to use papers that are natural, renewable and recyclable
products and made from wood grown in sustainable forests. The logging
and manufacturing processes are expected to conform to the environmental
regulations of the country of origin.

HEADLINE PUBLISHING GROUP
An Hachette UK Company
338 Euston Road
London NW1 3BH

www.headline.co.uk
www.hachette.co.uk

one

Principal Figgins's office, Monday morning

Rachel Berry paused outside the door to Principal Figgins's office just long enough to straighten her kneesocks and smooth down the sides of her corduroy skirt. Her bright white button-down and pink-and-green argyle sweater-vest seemed to scream *overachiever* – not that Principal Figgins needed to be reminded that Rachel Berry was special. McKinley High wasn't the kind of high school where students wanted to stand out. And Rachel stood out.

'Good morning, Mrs Goodrich.' Rachel smiled her 1,000-watt smile at the dour-faced secretary in the outer office. Mrs Goodrich always smelled like cookie dough, and for some reason she was always scowling at Rachel, which seemed unfair. She should be happy to see someone who was not a juvenile delinquent enter the principal's office. 'Is Principal Figgins in?'

'Do you have an appointment, Rachel?' Mrs Goodrich's beady eyes stared down at Rachel over the tops of her tiny bifocals.

'No, but Principal Figgins told me he is always glad to see me.' Rachel breezed past Mrs Goodrich's desk, feeling a faint craving for cookies. As her penny loafers padded quietly across the worn industrial carpet and through the open door of the principal's inner office, she couldn't help thinking it was kind of sad when a principal couldn't even get hardwood floors. But Rachel wouldn't let the sadness of Principal Figgins's existence bring her down – not today. Maybe he was stuck in a crappy office in crappy Lima, Ohio, but Rachel Berry wasn't going to be here forever. Not if she had anything to say about it.

For Rachel, freshman year had been a bit of a failure. She had thought high school was going to be all about coming into her own and helping people around her realize what a truly incredible and talented person she was. Instead, every time she raised her hand to give the – always correct – answer in history class, her fellow classmates rolled their eyes; every time she went to the front of the room to answer – correctly – the algebra problem on the board, she'd be tripped; and whenever she volunteered to act out one of the parts – usually the lead – in whatever Shakespeare play they were reading in Mr Horn's English class, she'd be heckled. Only in Lima would someone be ridiculed for aspiring to get out of Lima.

But the culmination of her humiliation had been her failed campaign for class president. The poster board signs she'd made with such care, combining patriotic red, white, and blue stripes with her signature gold stars, were nearly of professional quality. But the signs, along with the catchy slogans she and her dads had come up with, had all been desecrated in varying ways by naysayers. Someone had taken a Sharpie and changed VOTE BERRY – SHE'S A STAR to VOTE BERRY – SHE'S BIZARRE. After the election, which popular Sebastian Carmichael had won, to no one's surprise, Rachel demanded a recount. Jessica Davenport, one of the official ballot counters, told Rachel that no candidate had ever lost by such a large margin. In the history of the school. She said they'd double-counted, just because they thought it was a mistake. It wasn't.

'Rachel. Good morning.' Principal Figgins looked up briefly from his desk. The window behind him looked out on the student parking lot in all its glory, with students hiding behind their cars to smoke the last puffs of their cigarettes. A group of football players was hovering around a couple of freshmen, probably threatening to lock them in the porta-potty near the stadium's bleachers. 'I'm very busy today. Someone poured ten gallons of blue raspberry Kool-Aid into the swimming pool, and the entire swim team is stained blue.' He sighed heavily. His slight Indian accent became more pronounced when he was flustered. As the daughter of two gay dads, Rachel appreciated the fact that Lima was surprisingly diverse, for the Midwest.

'I'm sorry for the interruption, Principal Figgins, but it's very important.' She gracefully sat down in one of the chairs facing his desk, trying to ignore the inelegant farting sound the leather padding made beneath her, and carefully crossed her legs. Yes, freshman year was behind her. Nothing but a distant bad memory.

'Yes, Rachel.' He rubbed the dark splotches beneath his eyes, and Rachel wondered momentarily if everything in his home life was okay. He never looked very happy. 'Why don't you just go ahead and tell me what it is?'

'As you know, Principal Figgins, McKinley High School has a sadly limited number of creative outlets for performance-minded students such as myself.' It was true. For as long as she could remember, Rachel's fathers had let her enroll in any sort of activity she wanted – tap and ballet and, briefly, hip-hop. Vocal training, piano lessons, acting lessons. Public speaking training. Improv. Pageantry. Anything that allowed Rachel to be onstage.

But once she got to high school, her options seemed to disappear. It was all politics in high school.

'Yes, well.' Principal Figgins pushed his hair back, showing his receding hairline. 'Budget cuts make that a very tricky subject. I'm not sure there's anything I can do.'

'But there is, sir.' Rachel believed that when people gave no as an answer, they were usually just too lazy to try and figure out how to say yes.

'Enlighten me, then.'

4

Rachel had prepared a whole speech this morning while she did thirty minutes on the elliptical trainer in her bedroom. She was a firm believer in holistic health. She woke up early each morning to do either a cardio workout or yoga. This routine helped keep her balanced. 'I realized that there is one underutilized outlet that's just being wasted away – and that I would like to be allowed to take over. The morning announcements.' She waved her arms in a flourish, as if she had just announced an Oscar winner.

'But Mrs Applethorpe has always...'

'I know, sir.' Mrs Applethorpe was the attendance officer who, each morning during first period, read the daily announcements with the enthusiasm of a mortician. 'But I thought it would be fair to let someone else give it a try. Someone who could really pep up the announcements.' It was hard to stay still in her seat when Rachel felt so close to success. What better way to make herself – and her amazing voice – known? It was the closest thing the school had to a radio broadcast. And it was a captive audience – no one could change the station on her! After all, many important celebrities had got their start in radio, like Ryan Seacrest. *Not that he's as talented as I am*, Rachel thought.

Principal Figgins leaned back in his chair. 'It's not a terrible idea. Mrs Applethorpe has been complaining about her vertigo acting up when she stands in front of the microphone.'

'Excellent!' Rachel exclaimed. Mrs Applethorpe's loss was her gain.

Principal Figgins nodded, pressing his lips into a warning line. 'You can start it on a trial basis only. Two weeks.' He glanced at his watch. 'You can start today, if you get over to the attendance office in time.'

Ten minutes later, Rachel adjusted the microphone and ran her hard-bristle brush through her dark hair. It didn't matter that no one could see her; she still wanted to be at her best. The setup was a little simple – the attendance office didn't have all the equipment she would have preferred to work with – but it was a start.

'Just push the red button and start reading off the sheet,' Mrs Applethorpe directed loudly as she backed out of the room with a handful of knitting.

'Thank you,' Rachel answered politely, grateful that Mrs Applethorpe was leaving the room. '*Da da da da da da da da daaaa*,' she sang quietly, warming up her voice. Butterflies fluttered madly in her stomach, and she could feel her blood pumping quickly through her veins. Every particle of her body felt alive, as if it were suddenly spring after a long, cold winter. This was what performing was all about.

She pushed the red button.

'Good morning, McKinley High. This is Rachel Berry bringing you the daily announcements.' She took a deep breath. 'I'd like to start off with a tune from the seminal musical classic that we all know and love, *Singin' in the Rain*.' In a second, she was belting out her rendition of 'Good Morning' – and as she sang, she imagined her words drifting through the loudspeakers of every classroom, every student in school enthralled by the beauty of her voice. She imagined them whispering, 'Who is that? Rachel Berry? I had no idea she was so amazingly talented!' There was no sign of Mrs Applethorpe coming in to interrupt Rachel's show. She was either spellbound by Rachel's voice or wrapped up in her knitting. Either way, Rachel knew a victory when she saw it.

When she finished singing, she quickly rolled into the list of announcements. 'And now for the news of the day. I hope you're all planning on coming to the fall music recital: Fall in Love with Music!' Rachel had wondered if she should sign up for it; she was worried the school wasn't ready yet to see her onstage in all her glory.

'Also, voting starts today at lunch for this year's homecoming king and queen.' *Boring*, she thought. Like the king and queen were ever a surprise. It was always the prettiest, blondest girl, and the handsomest, most Ken-doll-type guy. 'The king and queen will be announced and crowned at the highly anticipated homecoming dance, which will follow the homecoming football game next Friday night.

'I'd like to sign off this morning by awarding Rachel Berry's Gold Star of the Week – a very special award given each week to a person who has done something outstanding to improve life at McKinley High.' She'd thought of this last night, and it seemed to be an appropriate way to give back to the school. 'This week I'd like to award the gold star to...' – she paused for effect – 'myself, for taking over morning announcements and bringing them back to life.' She was glad Mrs Applethorpe wasn't listening. Maybe it was a little much to give herself the first gold star, but she was doing the school a big service. And what was wrong with giving herself a little pat on the back when no one else was? 'I hope I've made everyone's morning a little brighter. See you all tomorrow!'

She pushed the OFF button and stared at the microphone. Her fingers were tingling from her success. She'd done it! She'd taken the first huge step of the year to becoming someone people actually knew and admired. Who knew? Maybe by next year, people would be voting for her for homecoming queen. The thought gave her chills.

Rachel slung her backpack over her shoulder as she left the attendance office. The hallway was packed with students clanking their lockers open and guys doing that shoulder-thumping thing they did. She had just a few minutes to get to her locker before first period. Her face was flushed with excitement. She felt like a new woman.

But...no one seemed to be looking at her. She stared at the students as they continued to brush past her, oblivious to the fact that she'd just given an amazing performance over the loudspeaker. Was it possible that everyone was just too jealous of her obvious talent to acknowledge her? The thought made her feel a little better.

She looked up to see Sue Sylvester, the hardened coach of the Cheerios. Rachel stood up a little straighter. She didn't exactly like Coach Sylvester, but part of her admired the woman for making the most of her situation. Having to settle for being a high school cheerleading coach was probably a big letdown, but Coach Sylvester had turned the cheerleading program at McKinley into one of the best in the state, taking the Cheerios to nationals twelve years in a row. The trophy cases that lined the walls of the main hallways were overflowing with gold-plated cheerleader statuettes.

'I hope you're prepared to be eaten alive by your fellow students for that disgusting little display of self-promotion this morning.' Coach Sylvester hitched her thumbs into the pockets of her red jogging suit.

'What?' Rachel blurted, but Coach Sylvester was already walking away. 'If I'm not my own advocate, who will be?' Rachel called after the coach.

'Here's a gold star for you,' Rachel heard someone say as she turned around, but all she saw was a blur of football players before the icy red splash of a slushie hit her in the face. The boys' laughter trailed down the hallway as they kept walking.

Deep breath. Getting slushied was nothing new. Those football guys could learn to be more creative. She'd been slushied at least a dozen times last year; she kept a change of clothes in her locker for just that reason. *Nice try, boys, but you'll have to work a little harder to bring Rachel Berry down this year.*

And at least they'd listened to her broadcast.

9

Things are about to change, she thought as she strode toward her locker, ignoring people's stares as the cold liquid dripped down her neck. It was going to be a big couple of weeks at McKinley High, and she was going to be at the center of it.

After she changed into a clean sweater.

two

McKinley High cafeteria, Monday lunch

The smell of undercooked Tater Tots and watery macaroni and cheese wafted from the kitchen of the McKinley High cafeteria as the student body rushed into the lunchroom. The popular students – the Cheerios, the jocks, and the beautiful and/or rich kids who wore expensive jeans – clustered around the most coveted cafeteria real estate, the tables near the long wall of windows that overlooked the courtyard. The football players, with their characteristic brio, squirted milk through straws and lobbed pieces of canned fruit at one another in their continued efforts to dominate the animal kingdom. They believed they were at the top of the food chain, and everyone else agreed.

'I can't eat this food,' one of the cheerleaders moaned as

she waved her fork in the air. A piece of spongy macaroni dangled from the tines. 'It's like I'm on a forced diet.'

'Coach Sylvester did say you looked a little sluggish on your flips,' the girl next to her whispered. 'Maybe it's not a bad idea.'

The tables in the middle of the cafeteria were taken up by various middle-of-the-road groups – the wannabes, closest to the popular kids, eyeing them enviously. The tables along the wall were home to the more ostracized groups – the Goths, the band geeks, the kids who picked their noses in class, and, in the farthest corner, near the tray return, the Glee kids. Tina Cohen-Chang, a pretty Asian-American girl with a blue streak in her shiny dark hair, spooned some blueberry yogurt into her mouth and tapped her foot on the floor as she hummed the latest Lady Gaga tune. 'Did you see that terrible girl on *Idol* last night? The one with the jazz version of "Imagine"?'

Kurt Hummel flicked his hair out of his face. 'John Lennon rolled over in his grave.' His eyes scanned the cafeteria. He didn't love sitting in the back, away from all the beautiful people, but it seemed that McKinley High was not ready for him. He was the best-dressed kid in school, but that didn't stop him from getting thrown in the Dumpster by guys who had never even heard of Alexander McQueen. If he leaned to the left just enough, he could see Finn Hudson's head as he devoured a slice of greasy cafeteria pizza. Oh, to be a greasy pepperoni on that piece.

'Oh no, they're not,' Mercedes Jones squealed, elbowing Tina in the ribs and pointing. Mercedes, one of a handful of African-American students at McKinley, sometimes felt like an outsider and was defensive. 'Those Cheerios are *charging* for homecoming votes!'

Tina and Kurt turned in the direction indicated by Mercedes's accusatory finger. Smack in the middle of the cafeteria, head Cheerio Quinn Fabray and her two slightly less pretty sidekicks, Santana and Brittany, had hijacked a table and turned it into a voting booth. A giant sign on a piece of Day-Glo pink poster board read VOTE FOR HOMCOMING KING AND QUEEN: $1 A VOTE! SPONSORED BY THE CHEERIOS. The girls, in their crisp cheerleading uniforms and matching glossy lips, were doing a brisk business, with eager students handing over the change from their lunch money for the privilege of filling out one of the homecoming ballots.

'Charging for votes?' Mercedes snorted. 'That's how they tried to hold down people in the South back in the day. They didn't get away with it then, so how can they do it now?'

'Are you g-g-going to go over there?' Tina asked, nervously chewing on her fingernail. She hated confrontation.

Mercedes sighed. She leaned back in her chair and chomped on a slice of green apple. 'What's the point?'

'Is that that Rachel girl from the announcements?' Kurt tapped Mercedes on the arm and pointed in the direction of the voting booth.

Rachel Berry, now de-slushied and wearing a navy blue

V-neck sweater that was only slightly crumpled from being stashed on the top shelf of her locker, approached the Cheerios table.

The sight of people handing over dollar bills to Quinn Fabray for their God-given right to vote made Rachel feel slightly sick – or maybe it was the sight of the congealed pieces of mac and cheese that someone had flung against the plate-glass courtyard windows. Some of the pasta had slid down the window, leaving behind a slimy trail.

'Two things,' Rachel said, stepping in front of a freshman girl in a Victoria's Secret pink sweatshirt. 'First, you spelled *homecoming* wrong on your sign.'

Quinn raised her eyes from the pack of money in her hands. She immediately felt her back straighten. Who the hell was Rachel Berry, one of the biggest losers to ever walk the halls of this school, to talk to her that way? Quinn only knew her name because she'd copied off her world history midterm last year in Mr Prospero's class. She opened her mouth to say something scathing in response, but Brittany, who was too blond for her own good, spoke up instead.

'What's the second thing?' she asked, tilting her head to the side as if she had water in her ear.

'We don't care what the second thing is,' Quinn interrupted. She stood up so that Rachel wasn't able to look down on her. 'Now, if you don't mind, kindly step aside and let the people you cut ahead of in line vote.'

'The second, and more egregious, thing,' Rachel said in a

louder voice, 'is that you're *charging* people to vote. It's hardly fair!' While she loved to be the center of attention, that wasn't why she was challenging the Cheerios. She just couldn't stand there and watch as they made everyone else do exactly what they wanted.

Quinn could practically feel the steam rising out of her ears. 'Maybe if you didn't spend so much on your librarian-meets-preschooler ensembles, you might be able to buy yourself enough votes to win. And then you could shut up.'

'But that would take a lot of votes,' Santana Lopez spoke up, eyeing Rachel's outfit. 'A whole lot.'

Brittany and the kids clustered around the table started to giggle nervously, and Rachel took a step backward. She opened her mouth to say something, but her mind was a blank. Why was it she could never think up the perfect comeback until an hour after she needed it?

But this time, she didn't need one. 'Excuse me, coming through.' Elbowing through the crowd to her rescue was ... Kurt Hummel? Kurt, wearing an asymmetrical kelly green sweater with buttons down one arm, pulled his black leather Gucci wallet out of his back pocket. He was tired of Quinn Fabray and her pretty, plastic friends bossing everyone around just because their pores were invisible and their breasts were perky and their hair stayed in place even as they did cartwheels during the halftime show. He pulled out a crisp fifty-dollar bill and tossed it carelessly onto the table. 'I'd like fifty votes for queen, please.'

15

Quinn made a face. 'For who?' She glanced around help-lessly, as if to say, *How could anyone be expected to deal with this?* 'You?'

The whole cafeteria seemed to burst into laughter. Rachel hadn't noticed how many people were actually watching the scene play out. She flipped her hair – flattened from her encounter with the slushie – behind her ears. Without thinking, she snatched back the fifty-dollar bill Kurt had tossed on the table. She didn't know what the hell he was doing, but it wasn't worth fifty dollars. He was already walking away with the confidence of someone who has made his point, his shoulders thrown back proudly, and the idea of adding anything else to the Cheerios' already oversaturated coffers made her apprehensive.

Rachel followed him out into the hallway, ignoring the stares of people over their half-eaten lunches. She didn't mind being stared at, or even laughed at. It was better than being ignored. But even so, it was nice to have someone else stand up behind you, even if it didn't totally make sense.

'You didn't have to do that!' Rachel called after him, her words echoing in the empty hallway. She strode up to him quickly and held out the fifty-dollar bill.

Kurt eyed the money for a moment before grabbing it with his thumb and forefinger. 'I guess this means neither of us will be queen.'

Rachel smiled. She had to respect Kurt for managing to be so confident even though he was such an outsider. Rachel was always seeing him climb out of the Dumpster by the parking lot after the football guys had tossed him in. He'd dust himself off, straighten his clothes, and go on with his day. Quinn Fabray, head of the almighty Cheerios, had practically called him gay in the crowded cafeteria, and he hadn't even seemed flustered. 'You know,' she said, hiking her backpack on her shoulder, 'my two dads had to go through the same kind of thing when they were in high school.'

Kurt's blue eyes narrowed slightly. 'You have two dads?'

'They're great.' Rachel nodded. 'Sometimes I forget that not everyone has two dads.'

Kurt eyed her thoughtfully. She thought maybe he was going to say something about being gay, but instead he said, 'I heard you sing on the announcements this morning.' He pursed his lips and looked as though he was debating what to say. 'You were actually okay.'

Okay? For some reason, this sounded like a huge compliment coming from Kurt. And since she hadn't actually been showered with compliments for her performance this morning – the slushie and a few eye rolls were all she'd got – her heart started to soar. 'Thank you,' she said, with uncharacteristic modesty.

'You might be interested in what Glee is doing these days. Stop by the choir room after school and check us out.' By *us*, she knew he meant the Asian-American girl with the stutter and Mercedes Jones. But if Glee was actually a club again, there must be more members. 'Oh, I don't know. I

17

spoke to Mr Ryerson last year about joining Glee. He made it clear that I would never get a solo – he said something about the importance of having only male soloists. Anyway, I got the sense that he doesn't appreciate true talent when he hears it,' Rachel said.

'True, Mr Ryerson isn't exactly the most inspiring Glee Club faculty adviser,' Kurt responded. 'But don't worry. He's never around. In fact, the next couple of weeks he's *really* not around. Apparently our pastel-clad fearless leader is attending Ohio's annual doll collectors' convention. Anyway, we'll be practicing this afternoon and, to be honest, we could use some more talent.'

'I'll have to check my schedule,' Rachel bubbled. 'But, yeah, maybe I'll think about it.'

Kurt's blue eyes stared her down. 'Maybe I'll see you later.'

'Maybe,' Rachel said as he walked away. She tried to wipe the smile off her face. It would be interesting to check out this group and see what they could do.

Back in the cafeteria, the clamor around the voting table had been replaced by an orderly stream of voters. Quinn poked Brittany in the ribs. 'Great job on the sign. It might have been more effective if you'd spelled all the words correctly.'

Brittany blinked and took a carrot stick from the small Tupperware container on her lap. 'You know I hate grammar.'

'Spelling isn't grammar,' Quinn responded, but there was no point with Brittany. Of course, Quinn should have known better than to leave something important to her. 'I'll fix it,' Quinn snapped, grabbing a black marker from her bag. She waited until there was a lull in the voting before hopping onto the table. The entire cafeteria was going to try to look up her short cheerleading skirt, but let them look at her bloomers. She was the president of the Celibacy Club, after all, and they could look all they wanted. They just couldn't have it. Quinn popped the cap off the marker and quickly wedged an E into HOMCOMING.

'It's a little crooked,' Finn Hudson said as Quinn took a tiny step back to admire her work. 'But it looks good.'

Quinn glanced down at Finn. 'Thanks.' He was gorgeous, all right, in that all-American, apple-pie-eating way. When Quinn was eight and picturing her wedding, complete with a Vera Wang princess dress in pale pink and ten thousand white tulips lining the aisle, the groom looked exactly like Finn. He was so tall that, even standing on the table, Quinn didn't feel like she was towering over him, and his light brown hair was always rumpled in the same boyish way.

Quinn held out her hand. 'Help me down.' Santana was staring at her. Quinn knew that practically every girl at McKinley had some level of crush on Finn. But it was too bad for them, because Quinn had recently decided that this was the year she'd become Finn Hudson's girlfriend. Or, more accurately, this was the year that she would allow Finn to become Quinn Fabray's boyfriend.

Finn grinned. Instead of grabbing her hand and helping

19

her step down onto the chair she'd used to climb up, Finn simply reached up and grabbed her around the waist. He swept her off the table and held her for a moment before setting her feet down on the orange linoleum floor.

'Not exactly what I meant, but thanks.' Quinn giggled, then lowered her eyes and looked up at Finn through her thick lashes. Quinn and Finn. Finn and Quinn. Maybe it was a little too Dr Seuss-y, but it made sense. Finn Hudson was easily the best-looking guy in the school, and he was also the star quarterback – if you could use the word *star* when talking about a team that had lost every one of its preseason games. But that hardly mattered. And Quinn had worked so hard to impress Coach Sylvester and become head Cheerio.

If she and Finn were an official couple, they'd be shoo-ins for homecoming king and queen. Quinn was already planning to wear her hair in a way that wouldn't get messed up when Principal Figgins or whoever announced the winners placed the plastic tiara on her head.

'You look like you've been really busy. I mean, collecting votes and all.' Finn had a habit of staring at his feet when he talked, just glancing up when he reached the end of his sentence. It was endearing, but Quinn kind of wished he'd be a little more confident.

'A Cheerio's duties are never done,' Quinn quoted Coach Sylvester. She glanced over Finn's shoulder, and her gaze landed on Puck Puckerman, Finn's teammate and one of his best friends. Puck was always doing something he shouldn't do, and now he'd fashioned a slingshot out of two pencils and a rubber band and was trying to aim a grape at someone at the other end of his table. He looked stupid with his silly Mohawk carved into what would have been beautiful, glossy black hair. But, still, there was something about him. Sex appeal, her mother might have called it if she were talking about a movie star. Puck exuded it. Something raw and dangerous that made Quinn shiver whenever she thought about being alone with him.

'What are you doing after school?' she heard Finn ask, and she dragged her eyes from Puck before Finn finished his sentence and his big puppy-dog eyes met hers.

'Practice, as usual.' Somehow Quinn's eyes were magnetically drawn back to Puck. This time, however, he seemed to sense it, and a cocky half grin came across his face before Quinn could look away. Great. He was definitely going to tease her about that later, and she would have to pretend he'd imagined it all. Quinn felt her face flush, but she recovered quickly.

She turned to Finn and put her hand on his bare arm. 'What are you doing tomorrow? Will you come to Celibacy Club with me after Cheerios practice? Maybe we could go out for frozen yogurt afterward.' Quinn was tired of waiting for Finn to make a move, so she'd decided to just ask him out herself. Though they'd been friends for the past year, Quinn and Finn weren't a couple, and Quinn was ready to lose her single status for a while. After all, a queen needs her king.

'Yeah, I'd like that.' Finn couldn't get over the feel of Quinn's warm palm on his arm. It was worth putting up with Celibacy Club, Quinn's second-favorite after-school activity. Going to a Celibacy Club meeting didn't sound fun at all, but it was a small price to pay to get to spend some time with Quinn. She was the hottest girl in school, even if she could be a little harsh sometimes. But the competitive edge she got from all that time spent with the Cheerios had probably made her so driven. And her lips – they were heart-shaped and looked like the softest lips Finn had ever seen. He'd be crazy not to be into her, and Finn Hudson was a lot of things, but crazy wasn't one of them.

three

Choir room, Monday after school

After school on Monday, the hallways of McKinley High emptied out as students scuttled off to extra-curricular activities, sports practices, or, in the case of McKinley's many underachievers, detention. The choir room, across the hallway from the auditorium, was empty except for the remaining members of the Glee Club: Mercedes, Tina, Kurt, and Artie Abrams, one of the few McKinley students in a wheelchair. The large room, lined with thick soundproofing materials, had tiered platforms designed for optimal acoustic quality. During the day, the choir room was inhabited by the band geeks, who were, for some unknown reason, seen as higher on the social totem pole than the Glee kids. Lining the walls were lockers in which students could store their musical instruments, and the shelves were filled with sheet music. A blackboard on the front wall listed the marching band's set list for the upcoming football game – 'We Will Rock You', 'Another One Bites the Dust', and the main theme from *Star Wars* – as well as the jazz band's practice schedule: THIS WEEK: MONDAY THRU FRIDAY, 6:30 AM. And at the very top of the board, in big letters, it read: FALL IN LOVE WITH MUSIC RECITAL: THIS FRIDAY. A shiny black grand piano sat on the floor next to a full drum set, the drumsticks sitting on the round black stool, waiting to be used.

The evidence of the thriving band program seemed only to highlight the paltriness of the Glee program, which had devolved over the years from a group of several dozen kids to the four students in the room. Since its glory days in the 1990s, when McKinley High had been a regular threat at regionals and sectionals, Glee Club had fallen on hard times. With budget cuts and little student interest, the role of staff supervisor for Glee had become something of a joke. It had been handed off from teacher to uninterested teacher, and under creepy Sandy Ryerson's mostly apathetic guidance, the club had virtually disappeared.

That is, except for the handful of students who were still willing to spend time after school, risking further social censure, just to sing.

Unfortunately, the group of four wasn't exactly meshing. As Mercedes, the most accomplished singer, belted out the lyrics to *West Side Story*'s 'Tonight', the others hummed and sang backup vocals, but something was missing. It wasn't that they were *bad*. They weren't. Tina had a lovely alto, even if she lacked confidence. Amazingly, Kurt could hit a high F. And Artie's voice was deep and rich. They just weren't *enough*.

'We sound like a bunch of amateurs,' Kurt announced after Mercedes's voice trailed off, vocalizing what everyone was thinking. He stuck his hands into the back pockets of his gray skinny jeans. 'No offense, Mercedes,' he quickly added, seeing her face cloud over. 'It's not you. You're awesome.'

'I know.' Mercedes cleared her throat and stared out the window at a group of boys in soccer shorts tossing a Frisbee. 'We're just…not clicking.'

'We're running out of time,' Tina reminded the group, although no one had forgotten. They all could see the huge letters looming at the top of the blackboard. 'The show is on Friday.'

'We're going to be humiliated. Further.' Artie rolled his wheelchair around in a giant circle. The collar of his white button-down shirt was stained blue. 'I got slushied twice this morning.'

'That's just wrong.' Kurt shook his head knowingly. The jocks in this school were animals. Strong, sinewy, sweaty animals.

'We just need to get it together,' Mercedes announced, clapping her hands. She'd been singing in her church's choir since she was eight, and she could bring tears to the eyes of the crankiest old lady with her rendition of 'Amazing Grace'.

She was the shining star of the Glee Club, and she'd be damned if she was going to be humiliated in front of her peers. The other kids in Glee were great, too – at least, individually. They just needed a little extra something to tie it all together. They would just have to keep singing until their tongues fell off. 'Take it from the top. Again.'

'Again?' Tina moaned, sinking down into a chair. She loved singing, but she wasn't sure about doing it in front of the entire school. She'd agreed to do the show only because everyone else wanted to do it, but now she was having second thoughts. 'We need more than practice.'

'Yeah, we need to stop whining and just get it right. I'm definitely not going to make a fool of myself onstage.' Mercedes shot a piercing glare at each one of them. 'Are you with me?'

They started again. Halfway through the song, which had improved slightly with this round, the door to the choir room flew open, clanking loudly against a rack of music stands. In the doorway stood Rachel Berry, looking like she'd stepped out of an episode of *The Brady Bunch* in her corduroy skirt, collegiate sweater, and kneesocks. The grin on her face stretched from ear to ear. The sight was so unexpected – for everyone except Kurt – that all the Glee members stopped singing, their voices trailing off into silence.

Not for long. 'That was a fairly reprehensible rendition of a Broadway classic. Artie, you were flat; Kurt, you were sharp. And girl whose name I don't know yet' – she pointed at Tina – 'you need to actually open your mouth when you sing. And Mercedes…' She trailed off when she saw the look on Mercedes's face.

'Oh no, you don't,' Mercedes replied, hand on her hip. She took a step forward, as if she were about to tackle Rachel. 'Who died and made you Simon Cowell?'

'Are those sequins on her kneesocks?' Tina whispered to Artie, eyeing Rachel's white kneesocks. They were, indeed, trimmed with gold sequins. 'And she's giving *us* advice?' Still, Tina made sure she opened her mouth when she said it. She knew she had a problem with enunciation.

Rachel remained unflustered. She plastered a bright yet determined smile on her face and stepped into the room, her ballet flats smacking gently against the linoleum floor. 'After much consideration, I've decided to join you in Glee Club, even though I've had professional vocal training practically since birth and am overqualified for anything this school can offer.' She paused while the room remained silent. 'And after hearing that travesty you call a performance, I'm confident that I'm exactly what you need to take you to the top.'

Tina and Artie glanced at each other in confusion, and Kurt nervously ran his hand through his hair, ruining the carefully sculpted look he'd spent twenty minutes perfecting in front of the bathroom mirror, one spray of Frédéric Fekkai aerosol hair spray at a time. Had he been so blinded by her talent that he'd forgotten completely that Rachel Berry was an irritating, brown-nosing know-it-all who had an almost intuitive way of alienating every person in the room? Had he made a huge mistake by inviting her to the rehearsal?

He glanced at Mercedes, who was looking Rachel up and down with an unamused look. In fact, she looked positively pissed. 'I don't know who you think you are, Little Miss Pink Heart-Shaped Barrettes, but you're not our coach, and no one invited you here, so maybe you should just shut your mouth and stroll back to your Disney movie.'

'Actually...' Kurt took a deep breath and faced the group. 'I invited her.'

Mercedes blinked. '*What?*' She stared at him as if he'd just told her he'd killed her puppy.

'Look, we've got to face it. We suck. Glee is pretty much dead, anyway, unless we do something to save it.' He fingered the gold watch he'd inherited from his maternal grandfather. 'We heard Rachel sing this morning on the PA, and while I'm sure we'd all admit that her self-promotion was startlingly transparent, she *was* incredible.'

'Thank you,' Rachel replied primly. She had learned by now to ignore the backhanded parts of compliments and focus only on the positive. With a career in show business in front of her, that was the only way to do it.

Kurt nodded briefly toward her. He found it slightly shocking that someone so interested in the performing arts could have such terrible style. The kneesocks were atrocious. 'Although she may not be what we're used to, I think Rachel is the obvious solution to our problem.'

'I can't believe this,' Mercedes cried out, rubbing her temples. She stared at Kurt. Suddenly, in his charcoal-gray cashmere turtleneck and slim-fitting gray pants, he looked like a stranger to her. Kurt thought she wasn't good enough? He was supposed to be her friend. She felt as if he'd slushied her pride.

'Mercedes, you're awesome, d-d-don't get us wrong.' Tina was surprised to find herself speaking up. She thought Rachel had sounded really good that morning, too. Way better than Mrs Applethorpe's monotonous drone. Tina realized that it might be good for her to be around someone who was so bold and confident. Maybe it would help her overcome some of her shyness. 'But we need more than one really strong singer. We need someone who can make all of us better.'

Mercedes narrowed her eyes. That morning in homeroom, when she heard Rachel sing over the loudspeaker, she'd thought, *Damn, that white girl can sing*. Mercedes tried to picture the four of them, with no Rachel, performing on the stage in front of the entire school at the Fall in Love with Music recital. Short of some miracle, it was going to be a total disaster. Maybe, just maybe, the solution was standing in front of them in an annoyingly short skirt and sparkly socks. She took a deep breath. 'Okay. She can stay.'

Rachel nodded. She wanted to remind Mercedes that she didn't exactly *need* her permission, but for once she held herself back.

Mercedes glared at her. 'For now.'

'You won't be sorry.' Rachel sat down on the piano bench and ran her fingers along the keys. 'From what I've heard, we need to get serious. Enough baby steps. It's not going to be all easy, and it's not going to be all fun. But if you really want to improve, you need to follow my lead. And we're going to need to practice here every day after school, until the show.'

Mercedes raised an eyebrow. This was going to be an adventure.

four

Mr Schuester's Spanish II class, Tuesday morning

Tina turned around in her seat. 'All I could think about last night was how much better we sounded when she sang with us,' she admitted to Artie before the start of Mr Schuester's Spanish II class on Tuesday morning. It was the first period of the day, and one of Tina's favorites. Talking to Artie first thing in her morning made it easier to get through a whole day of teasing. Artie was sweet. And she liked looking at the giant poster that hung on the wall next to her desk: the Picasso ink drawing of Don Quixote on his skinny horse.

'If only her personality was a little less...' Artie trailed off. He sat at the last desk in the first aisle, the only one that was wheelchair-accessible. He wanted to be diplomatic about

Rachel. He was pretty sure she wasn't a completely horrible person, but she just managed to come off that way. His mom had always told him to say only nice things about people, but that policy wasn't always practical.

'Bossy?' Tina commented, drawing an upside-down skull on the cover of Artie's notebook. 'Annoying? Offensive?' Rachel had told her that she enunciated like a two-year-old, which Tina didn't think was fair. She had a speech impediment, all right?

Artie straightened his black-framed glasses and stared at the list of vocabulary words Mr Schu was going to quiz them on today. 'I was thinking *loud*, but those work, too.'

Their discussion was silenced by the staticky feedback that came over the loudspeaker whenever someone turned on the mike. 'Let's see what she does today,' Tina whispered, turning forward in her seat to face the blackboard, where the word *ser* had been incorrectly conjugated by someone on the previous day. Mr Schuester hadn't noticed it. Next to the writing, a giant map of Spain was halfway unrolled over the blackboard.

'Happy Tuesday morning, McKinley High!' Rachel's cheerful voice boomed into every classroom. 'It's Rachel Berry here, bringing you the morning announcements. In sports news, the boys' soccer team led a valiant effort against Troy High, but unfortunately the team was defeated in the final seconds of the game. You'll get them next time, boys!'

'Is it wrong to want to murder someone for being too

cheerful?' Tina asked over her shoulder as Rachel announced, with almost unnatural enthusiasm, the results of the senior government class's mock trial.

'I think so.' Artie had meant to tell Tina he liked her LITTLE MISS GROUCHY T-shirt when he first saw her in the hall that morning, but he was afraid she'd think he was staring at her boobs. Was it too late to tell her now?

'And now I'd like to bring to your attention a disturbing case of injustice that is going on right here at McKinley High,' Rachel continued. Artie and Tina exchanged a worried glance. Had Rachel gone completely off the rails? 'Those of you who tried to do your civic duty and vote for homecoming king and queen were probably shocked and appalled to find that certain cheerleaders running the voting booth were *charging* people to vote.'

A few students chuckled. 'As anyone who has taken Mr Hillburger's American history class knows, the Twenty-fourth Amendment prohibits the practice of charging a citizen to place his or her vote. If it's good enough for the Constitution of the United States of America, I think it's good enough for McKinley High. If this were happening in Iran, CNN would be running headline stories about it, but because pretty blond girls are doing it here, at our high school, everyone hands over dollar bills.'

'Is she insane?' Artie whispered. 'She sounds like a CNN news update.'

'I don't think it's that f-f-far-fetched to assume there's

something psychologically wrong with her,' Tina whispered back. 'Like, clinically.'

Rachel's pert voice continued. 'In conclusion, I urge you all to boycott the homecoming election because of its blatant unfairness. I'm sure—'

'I don't know who you think you are.' A deep, brash voice interrupted Rachel's plea. The entire school immediately recognized it as the voice of Sue Sylvester, the legendary coach of the Cheerios. She was powerful and opinionated and known for kicking Cheerios off the squad if they cried in public. 'But you are way out of line here. Challenging the status quo is a deceitful and insidious tactic.'

Artie leaned forward. 'This is getting good,' he whispered to Tina. The whole class leaned forward in their desks, eagerly listening to the exchange on the loudspeaker. Most people knew not to mess with Coach Sylvester, but Rachel seemed oblivious to that sort of thing.

'I wish there was video,' Tina answered. Secretly, though, she worried that people would take seriously Rachel's call to boycott the homecoming election and might even boycott the dance itself. Tina was kind of hoping that Artie would ask her to the dance, even though she knew it was silly. Artie got nervous about things like that, and going to a school dance was probably the last thing he wanted to do. Still...

'Charging students to vote is unethical and...' There was a nervous note in Rachel's voice as she spoke to Coach Sylvester.

'I'll tell you what unethical is. Unethical is you denying my Cheerios the right to raise money for their tanning needs. These are some talented athletes who are going all the way to the top, and you, young lady, need to stick to your lonely path to unrealized ambitions.'

Everyone in the classroom burst into laughter. 'If Rachel's starting a fight with Coach Sylvester, she's even crazier than we thought,' Artie said, shaking his head.

'I don't know.' Tina smiled and glanced out the window. It was a sunny day, and the smell of freshly mowed grass came through the open window. Maybe what Glee needed was someone who was willing to fight for it. 'Maybe we should just stick it out for a while. At least until the performance on Friday.' She shrugged. Maybe *she* was the crazy one, but she felt they might actually have a chance to sound good in front of the whole school. 'Then we'll know once and for all if Glee is doomed.'

'I hope it's not.' Artie leaned back in his chair. Rachel was still bickering with Coach Sylvester. He couldn't imagine life in high school without Glee after school. He got to hang out with Tina and sing and be someone besides 'that wheelchair kid'. There, he was a baritone, someone who could sing the low parts, someone who did a mean rendition of Usher's 'OMG'. He was part of something, not just a single odd piece that didn't fit in. There, he was normal. 'Glee is the best part of my day.' His dark eyes met hers for a moment before returning to his list of conjugated Spanish verbs.

Tina blushed. That was exactly how she felt. 'I...I,' she stammered, having a hard time starting. 'I know what you mean,' she said finally.

Artie nodded. 'So if Rachel can help us keep it going, I'm willing to make certain allowances, like putting up with her awful personality.'

'And I'll leave you with a musical note in honor of today,' Rachel's voice came over the PA. Coach Sylvester had stormed out of the room in a huff, probably vowing to get back at Rachel 'and your little dog, too'. In a clear, confident voice, Rachel began to sing a verse from an old Rolling Stones song, 'Ruby Tuesday'.

Having taught almost ten years at a middle-of-the-road high school deep in the farmland of central Ohio, Mr Schuester was fairly good at zoning out when one of his kids started rambling on. That morning, he'd found himself daydreaming about running a bed-and-breakfast in Bali, and he hadn't heard the majority of Rachel Berry's morning announcements. On paper, she was the kind of student any teacher should love, but in the flesh she left something to be desired. The previous year, in Spanish II, Rachel raised her hand so often that Mr Schuester had to turn his desk in a different direction so that she wouldn't be in his direct line of vision. Her enthusiasm was, in some lights, charming, but in others, just an annoyance.

When she started singing 'Ruby Tuesday', though, Mr Schuester's ears perked up. Despite the poor acoustics of the announcement room microphone and the staticky PA system, it was clear that Rachel was good. Very good, even. For a second, listening to her voice took him back to his own days at McKinley High, back when Glee was full of talented, confident students who loved to perform in front of the entire school and who always brought down the house. He'd been one of the stars himself, and while he wouldn't say he could have had any girl he wanted, he'd definitely had his fans among female students. But it was always only about Terri, whom he'd married when they were both halfway through Ohio State.

'See you tomorrow,' Rachel signed off in her chipper voice. 'Remember to *not* vote.'

Smiling, Mr Schuester stood up. He gazed across the room at the rows of bored students, some chewing on pencils and some texting under their desks, as if he wouldn't notice. He'd planned a lesson on conjugating *-er* verbs today, but suddenly he decided to do something different. Something new and exciting.

'Guys, how would you like to learn the words to "Guantanamera"?' He felt inspired again, thinking about the days when he and his Glee friends would sing and jam together. Everything had seemed so much...happier then.

The students exchanged glances, as if this were a trick. 'Is that a song?' someone asked.

'Only the most popular song in the history of Cuba.' He cleared his throat and started singing. At first the students giggled and looked at him like he was crazy, but in a few minutes he could see them swaying in their seats, as if they couldn't fight the beat. A couple of cheerleaders in the back started clapping along. Feeling good, he did a couple of quick salsa-inspired moves, much to his students' amusement. He'd forgotten that dancing made a person feel good – although Terri claimed that dancing would give her lupus, which ran in her family. From the front of the classroom to the back, smiles lit up all the faces.

Mr Schuester smiled, too. He was reminded that teaching could be fun.

five

Football field, Tuesday after school

The vast, grassy sports fields that stretched out behind the high school always bustled with activity the second the final bell rang. Boys and girls wearing running shorts and McKinley Athletics Department T-shirts circled the school grounds and neighborhood streets for cross-country practice, and the soccer fields were filled with kids thundering across the grass, scrambling to get a foot on the ball. The football team had command of the centrally located football field, and the Cheerios held their practices in the far end zone. Tuesday afternoon was unseasonably warm, and all the teams – with the exception of Coach Sylvester's whip-trained cheerleading squad – were a little lazier in their efforts. The runners jogged a little slower, flirting with members of the opposite sex as they ran.

The football team, especially, in their uniforms and heavy pads, were moving sluggishly. Most of the players were stretched out on the field in various states of repose, pretending to have completed a drill when Coach Tanaka looked their way. The coach was in the near end zone, working with Daniel Duffy, the team's kicker, who had to this point managed to kick the ball through the goalposts on only one out of twenty-three tries. The rest of the team was under orders to run drills, but something in the warm air made everyone reluctant to move, and concentration seemed impossible.

Or maybe it was because the Cheerios were acting extra peppy at their end of the field, their girlish voices calling out instructions that the football guys couldn't understand. In the brilliant September sunlight, with their ponytails flipping as they executed their routines perfectly, they looked like birds. Lithe, acrobatic birds, Finn couldn't help thinking. He'd been throwing passes across the field to Puck Puckerman, but Puck kept dropping the ball because he was watching the girls as well.

'Dude, they are so hot.' Puck came up behind Finn and punched him in the shoulder pad. They'd been friends for years, since they played on opposing Little League teams. Puck had hit Finn in the head with a fastball. He'd insisted that Finn was crowding the plate, and Finn had rushed the mound. After the game Finn's mother took them out for ice cream, and all was forgiven. 'It's cruel and unusual punishment to make us try and practice while they're out there flipping their skirts up.'

'I know. They're really good.'

Both of them watched as Quinn Fabray started running. Each held his breath as she executed a perfect double flip before spiraling through the air in a move that looked as though it belonged in the summer Olympics. Quinn landed on her feet with an *oompf*, her ponytail bouncing at the end. She immediately returned to her original position without breaking a sweat. Did girls even sweat? Finn wondered. How come they never smelled like the boys' locker room after practice? He was pretty sure Quinn always smelled good.

'Quinn, huh?' Puck glanced at Finn. He took off his helmet and hung it at his side. 'You two going out?'

'I don't know. Kind of. I mean, I think that we're going to start hanging out soon.' Finn wiped the sweat off his forehead with his equally sweaty palm. He didn't really know why Quinn liked him, but he guessed she did, since she'd invited him to the Celibacy Club meeting and then out for ice cream. He'd always thought she was pretty, though, and once she started paying some attention to him, he felt that he should go with it. Only a crazy person would turn down Quinn Fabray. 'I'm going to Celibacy Club with her today.'

Puck raised his eyebrows. 'What's *that* all about?'

'I don't know,' Finn said again. 'I guess she's, uh, into it.'

Which was weird, because Quinn was totally hot, and she had this totally sexy way of talking in this kind of quiet voice that sounded so sweet and girly, even when she was bitching at someone. Like the other day at lunch, when she'd yelled at both Brittany and that Rachel Berry girl, and that poor dude that Puck and the other football players were always throwing in the Dumpster. Quinn seemed kind of angry a lot of the time.

But the way she had touched his arm when she asked him to Celibacy Club was so gentle, and it really had turned him on. He liked her. He really did. He was sure of it – or, at least, half-sure of it. It was just hard to tell. Puck was, like, the tenth guy to ask him about Quinn, and he was really feeling the pressure. If he didn't ask her to the homecoming dance, did that mean there was something wrong with him? Or her?

'You gotta be careful around those church girls,' Puck replied, his eyes watching Quinn as she climbed to the top of a pyramid of girls. 'They're all wild underneath.' It wasn't fair that Finn got first dibs on Quinn just because he was the quarterback. The team sucked, so how good a quarterback was he, really? Finn didn't even seem totally into her, which also wasn't fair, since Puck wanted her. Really badly.

She'd always been hot but a little too goody-goody for Puck to notice her. But on the first day of school this year, she'd sat in front of Puck in biology. When she lifted her arm and reached back to scratch her shoulder, the neckline of her shirt bunched up, and he caught a glimpse of her pale pink bra strap. Normally, the sight of a bra strap wasn't a big deal to Puck. After all, that summer he had started a thriving business cleaning aboveground pools, and his success was based mostly on his ability to please lonely older women who wore sexy underwear and lusted after him openly. His abs were ripped, and cougars dug his Mohawk.

But something about that peek at the pale pink strap against Quinn's tanned shoulder had gotten him all hot and bothered. Sometimes the image came back to him as he was running down the field or eating a slice of pizza or throwing a slushie into a freshman's face, and it was so vivid he'd swear he could smell her strawberry shampoo.

'I don't know,' Finn said, sounding disappointed. He grabbed a football and tossed it in the air. 'I don't think Quinn's like that.'

Across the field, after Brittany and Santana basket-caught Quinn from the top of the pyramid, Coach Sylvester blew the silver whistle she wore around her neck. 'Take five, ladies. No, take three. That pyramid was wobbly, and if you think we can make it all the way to the top with that, you are all sorely mistaken. You think this is hard? Try giving yourself laser eye surgery – *that's* hard.' She patted Quinn on the shoulder as she passed. 'Nice job, Q. That was as close to perfection as these lazy underachievers are going to get.'

'Thanks.' Quinn and Santana wandered to the bench and grabbed their water bottles. As Quinn threw her head back and took a long drink of sun-warmed water, she could still feel eyes on her from across the field. Finn and Puck had been staring at her for about ten minutes, and it made her feel good. Who didn't appreciate the adoring gazes of two hot guys? Her father had doted on her since she was a little girl, and Quinn found herself craving male attention. It made her sit up straighter, smile more sweetly, and put everything she had into her flips.

'Puck cannot keep his eyes off me today,' Santana proclaimed as she waved at Puck flirtatiously, tilting her hips to one side.

Are you delusional? Quinn wanted to say. *He's staring at me.* Instead, she just made a noncommittal *hmm* sound. But maybe Santana was right – maybe Puck wasn't watching Quinn after all. Santana was pretty, Quinn thought, but in an easy-girl kind of way. Everyone knew that Santana had made out with at least six guys last year. But, then, Puck was a player who was notorious for dating a girl for a week before dumping her and moving on to her best friend.

Why did Quinn even care what Puck thought about anything? He was one of those guys who skipped class and talked back to teachers and didn't care about getting out of Lima. Ten years from now, he'd probably have flunked out of Lima Community College and would be drinking cheap beers and sleeping on his mom's sofa. Total Lima loser material.

Well, Finn was certainly staring at her, anyway. And he was definitely a better catch. Maybe not the smartest guy in the world, but he was tall and handsome. That should be enough.

'He's totally going to ask me to the homecoming dance.' Santana pushed up the strap of her sports bra.

'Who?'

'Puck, obviously.' Santana glanced over her shoulder at him. 'I can just tell by the way he asked to cheat off my geometry homework this morning.'

'Really?' Quinn grabbed her ankle and pulled it toward her back to stretch out her quad. She glanced at the bleachers, not wanting Santana to see her face. A couple of trumpet players in the marching band were practicing for the home-coming game, but otherwise the bleachers were empty. The thought of Puck putting his hands on Santana's waist as they made out and swayed back and forth to some lame soft-rock song suddenly made her feel ill.

'Definitely.' Santana nudged her in the ribs. 'Are you okay? You look pale.'

'Dehydrated,' Quinn lied, dropping her ankle and grabbing her water bottle again.

'Oh.' Santana put her arm on Quinn's shoulder. 'I'm sure Finn's going to ask you, you know. He's been watching you for, like, an hour! And you'll totally make the cutest couple.'

'We will.' Quinn smiled. She could picture Finn showing up at the door to her giant house, holding some kind of corsage in the wrong color, grinning his goofy grin. 'We totally will.'

Later, when Coach Sylvester triple-tweeted her whistle, signaling the end of practice, Quinn tried not to watch as the football players headed to the locker room. Santana made a beeline for Puck, jogging over to him with her ponytail bouncing, and Quinn had to bite the inside of her cheek to keep from running over there and keeping them apart.

She knew she was being ridiculous. What was it about Puck, anyway? Was she just attracted to him because he was the bad-boy type? That was so lame. She gathered her things slowly, savoring the feeling of having finished a hard practice successfully. She loved the way her calves trembled with fatigue and her shoulders ached. It was good pain. All the Cheerios had rushed back to the locker room to change, and it was nice to have a moment alone. Football and soccer practices had ended, too, and the air was quiet. She threw her bag over her shoulder and headed past the bleachers, trying not to wonder whether Santana was still shamelessly flirting with Puck.

All of a sudden, someone grabbed her from behind and pulled her under the bleachers, into the alcove where all the upperclassmen made out during games. A tiny shriek escaped her lips before the strong hands turned her around and she saw who it was. Puck.

Her hazel eyes widened, and her stomach whooshed out from underneath her, the way it did at the top of the giant hill on the Iron Dragon roller coaster at Cedar Point. 'What the hell do you think you're doing?' Her bag slid off her arm and landed in the soft grass.

'What I've been thinking about doing all through practice. This.' Puck pinned her against a metal support beam and pressed his lips to hers before she could say or think anything.

His mouth was warm and surprisingly soft, his lips salty, and the warmth seeped into Quinn's body, starting at her own lips and spreading down to her fingertips and her toes. She was definitely going over the roller coaster hill.

Quinn pushed Puck away. She took a deep breath and straightened her practice skirt, trying to calm the butterflies in her stomach. The last boy she'd let kiss her was Andrew Atkinson, and that had been like kissing a gulping frog. Kissing Puck was...something different entirely. 'Who said you could do that?' She tilted her chin toward him rebelliously.

'You.' Puck grinned confidently. He smelled like sweat, but somehow on him it smelled good. 'I saw you staring back at me during practice. I thought I was going to miss my chance when Santana wouldn't stop yapping at me.'

The butterflies in her stomach were doing karate now. She couldn't believe he'd kissed her. 'I thought you were into her,' Quinn said, crossing her arms over her chest.

'You know I like you.' Puck stroked her bare arm with his finger, and Quinn could feel all the tiny arm hairs stand on end. 'Don't deny it, Quinn. You like me, too.'

She opened her mouth to tell him he was being ridiculous, but instead she found herself unable to think of anything but the way Puck's lips had tasted. Before she knew what she was doing, she leaned forward and kissed him on the mouth, and his lips opened eagerly. *My God*, she thought as he pressed her back against the support beam, his hand firmly on her waist. *This is what a kiss is supposed to be.* She felt like her brain was totally floating away and her body was completely taking over. She couldn't believe those were her hands running down the back of Puck's damp T-shirt, across his Mohawk – she'd always wondered what it felt like – as she pulled him closer. For some odd reason, he made her think of Juicy Fruit gum. She used to love the flavor so much, she wasn't able to chew it for long before she had to – she couldn't help it – swallow it. Puck was like Juicy Fruit. She just wanted to devour him.

'Oh, wait.' Quinn shoved Puck away suddenly. He stumbled backward. 'What *time* is it? I'm supposed to run a Celibacy Club meeting.'

'Blow it off.' Puck grabbed Quinn's arm and tried to pull her to him. Part of her wanted nothing more than to spend the rest of the afternoon hiding under the bleachers with Puck, kissing his amazing lips. But the rest of her knew she had to get back to reality.

'I can't.' She shook off Puck's hand. He stepped toward her, and she felt herself falling under his spell again. That couldn't happen. 'Besides, I invited Finn out afterward.'

Puck stepped away. 'But you're not...' His voice trailed off.

'Can't talk. I'm so late.' She grabbed her bag, threw it over her shoulder, and ran toward the school, leaving Puck alone beneath the bleachers staring after her. Even though her father had always called her a princess, she'd never felt so much like Cinderella, leaving the ball long before she wanted to.

six

McKinley High hallway, Tuesday after school

With his hair still wet from his post-practice shower, Finn Hudson slung his backpack over his shoulder and strolled down the hallway on his way to the Celibacy Club meeting. It always felt good to be done with football for the day. During the school day, Finn often found himself pumping his right arm through the air as if he were throwing the football to a wide receiver in the end zone, something he had to do to psych himself up for practice. Football was okay, but it didn't really excite him anymore. Maybe when he was a freshman and girls first started to pay attention to him whenever he wore his uniform. Seriously, they'd hang around outside the locker room after a game –

even a terrible game – waiting to get a chance to talk to him. It was pretty cool.

It wasn't like that anymore. He was always thinking about football. At home, he'd sometimes do his homework standing up so he could do calf raises and squats while he worked. When he *did* his homework. He worked even harder on the field – he was always one of the first guys at practice. It wasn't always fun, but he hoped all the work would pay off someday when a scout spotted him and offered him a free ride to a good school. It didn't even matter what school, as long as it included a ticket out of Lima.

'Hey, Finn, are you ready to crush Central in the big game next weekend?' As Santana Lopez, in her short red-and-black Cheerios practice uniform, brushed past him, her long dark hair tickled his arm.

'Uh, yeah. I guess.'

'Quinn said you were coming to Celibacy Club today.' Santana's sneakers squeaked as she walked down the hall next to him. 'Is it your first time?'

That seemed like a strangely inappropriate question when talking about Celibacy Club. 'Yeah, I've never been before.'

'Cool.' Finn followed Santana into room 212, his eyes mesmerized by the swish of her Cheerios skirt as she sashayed through the doorway. She wasn't as pretty as Quinn, but she had this really hot body. It seemed so natural to think about how hot girls were. In Celibacy Club, would he be told not to?

'We separate boys and girls for the first half hour,' Santana instructed, hopping up onto a desk. 'As soon as Quinn calls the meeting to order.'

Finn paused – he didn't see Quinn's silky blond hair anywhere. This meeting would be halfway tolerable only because he was going out with her afterward, and maybe she'd let him make out with her. Instead, the Celibacy Club meeting was populated with a handful of other Cheerios, whose arms Quinn must have twisted to get them there, as well as a bunch of dorky-looking guys who probably had the warped idea that being in the club would help them get laid. There were also a few freshman and sophomore girls in frumpy clothes who looked like they hated men.

Finn felt a headache developing. The room seemed over-heated, and he couldn't imagine what he was supposed to talk about with a bunch of guys for half an hour. A poster on the wall showed Miss Piggy and Kermit the Frog in wedding wear with the slogan WORTH THE WAIT.

'Do you think Quinn's okay?' a girl with mouse-brown hair asked Finn shyly. She was a freshman on the Cheerios squad. 'She's never late.'

'I don't know,' Finn answered, glancing over his shoulder. He *did* know that if she didn't show up, he was out of there. Then it hit him – this was the perfect excuse to leave. 'But, uh, I'll go look for her.' He quickly disappeared into the hallway, grateful for a few more moments of freedom.

Finn wandered halfheartedly through the now-empty hall-ways, glancing around for Quinn. He bent to take a drink from the fountain outside the auditorium. A piece of pink gum floated in the drain, but he ignored it. Just as the cold spray of water hit his lips, someone started to sing. Beautifully. He forgot to keep his mouth open, and the water splashed off his face.

Finn stood up and wiped his mouth. He walked toward the open auditorium door. A girl was singing an old-fashioned-sounding song, and it sounded beautiful.

He didn't talk about it, ever, but Finn really loved to sing. In the shower at home – even in the locker room if there weren't a lot of guys around – he was always singing. He tended to belt out early Springsteen songs while he lathered up with shampoo, and it was Air Supply as he rinsed off. When he was singing, he forgot about the muscle aches and cramps he got from being knocked around, like a bumper car, on the football field. When he sang, he felt like someone else.

Who was singing like that? It sounded almost like a record – the voice was so confident and skilled. Finn quietly stepped through the doorway and stood in the shadows of the auditorium.

In the middle of the stage, all alone, stood Rachel Berry.

Huh. She sat in the front row of his history class and always answered Mr Tucker's questions in a know-it-all voice, as though she was surprised he'd even bothered to ask. The football guys who clustered around Finn in class often flung bits of crumpled paper at her, trying to make it stick in her shiny hair. She always wore kneesocks and sweaters and plaid, as if she were attending a Catholic girls' school and everyone else had forgotten the dress code.

This girl onstage seemed like a completely different person. Yeah, Finn had heard her on the morning announcements, and her voice had sounded pretty good, but he hadn't actually put it together with the image of her yet. Finn was completely spellbound, watching as Rachel wove her way across the stage, singing her heart out as if the auditorium were full of thousands of awestruck fans. She sang as if the whole world were watching, and she looked like she was having the time of her life. Finn squinted, glancing around the auditorium to see if she really was singing to someone, but it was empty.

Rachel Berry looked really hot.

'*What you are, what you do, what you say...*' Rachel sang, stretching out her hand. Part of Finn wanted to reach out and take it. He didn't know what the hell was going on, but he felt like his insides were shaking as he listened to Rachel – like he was, crazily, falling in love...with her?

Rachel stopped singing, but the song hung in the air like an echo. She was murmuring softly to herself now, maybe commenting on her performance. Finn shook himself out of his trance. It was just Rachel Berry up there again, the girl in his history class. But now that he'd heard her sing, it was hard to imagine her with that know-it-all voice again.

Rachel hummed a little to herself as she stared out at the

53

empty auditorium. She'd nailed the song, which wasn't surprising, as she'd been singing since she was in diapers. When she closed her eyes and sang, she wasn't standing on the stage in the McKinley High auditorium. She was on the darkened stage of the biggest theater on Broadway, singing to thousands and thousands of mesmerized men and women with tears in their eyes (even the men!), and her name was the biggest one on the posters outside.

All she needed to do was whip the school's lame Glee Club – ignored and rejected over the years as people rushed off to cooler activities, like cheerleading and math club – into fine fighting shape. How hard could that be?

She opened her eyes. She saw Finn Hudson right away, standing next to the side stairs that led off the stage, staring right at her.

Her heart thumped. Had he been watching her the entire time? Finn Hudson, with the broad shoulders, those dreamy brown eyes, and that tiny beauty mark on his left cheekbone that made Rachel long to kiss it. Had he been *watching* her? She hadn't realized he even knew she existed, and now he had this strange look on his face like he…thought she was something special.

'Hi, Finn,' Rachel bubbled. She felt funny standing on the stage while he was down below. She stepped toward the stairs. 'What are you doing here?'

Finn's backpack banged against a drum set that was sitting, abandoned, in the orchestra pit. 'I was at this, uh, Celibacy

Club meeting…and, uh, I heard you from out in the hall.'
He gestured toward the hallway.

'Oh?' Rachel smoothed the sides of her pink-and-white plaid skirt. Finn Hudson was actually *talking* to her! Her pulse raced. Even though just seconds ago she'd imagined thousands of people watching her, she felt nervous when it was *him*. Of course, the first time he talked to her, he had to be telling her she was too loud. That was it, right? 'I'm done singing now. I'm sorry I disturbed you.'

'No, I didn't mean that. The meeting hasn't started yet.' Finn fidgeted and looked up at her shyly. 'I couldn't help stopping. I mean, you have an incredible voice.'

'*Oh.*' Rachel sounded relieved. 'Thank you. I've been told that before.' She walked down the stage steps, moving closer to Finn. She might not ever get the chance to talk alone with Finn Hudson again – he was so busy playing football and being popular, he probably couldn't afford to spend much time talking to people from Rachel's social stratum – and she wanted to get a good look at those eyes of his. She could never tell if they were brown or hazel or somewhere in between.

It felt weird to talk to Rachel, but Finn couldn't stop. 'I think it's really cool that you can just get up there and, you know, sing like that.' He shrugged. 'I could never do that.'

Rachel's eyes widened. She was at the bottom of the stairs, but she stayed on the first step, because Finn was super-tall and she didn't want him to think that her own five-foot-two frame was too diminutive for him. In case someday he grew tired of dating cookie-cutter blonds and wanted more of a challenge. 'I don't know. You go out every week on the football field and throw the ball at people, with everyone watching.'

'Yeah, but they all expect us to lose, anyway, so it's no big deal.' He looked up at the stage lights, which were nearly blinding. 'I guess there are bright lights on the field, too.'

Rachel inched closer to him. She could smell Irish Spring soap. She wondered what the boys' locker room was like after a practice and how all those guys could stand to shower together. 'Are you ready for the homecoming game?'

Finn groaned.

'It can't be that bad,' Rachel said. She couldn't believe her conversation with Finn Hudson was lasting this long. He'd already said, like, a hundred words to her.

'No, it's just…I get tired of talking about football.' Finn kind of hated that everyone associated him with football, as if he were The Quarterback and nothing else. Football had its moments, but it wasn't everything to him. There had to be more, right? 'It's just that it would, maybe, be nice to be good at something else. Something that means something. Like you and singing.'

Rachel shrugged, but her cheeks flushed with pleasure. She never got tired of compliments, but they seemed extra special coming from Finn. 'I was just practicing for the music recital on Friday. We already had Glee practice after school, but I

56

like the acoustics in here better.' Finn turned his head slightly, and the light caught his eyes – they were definitely brown, with tiny flecks of green in them. She opened her mouth to say something – what, she didn't know. The way he was looking at her made her nervous....

'What are you doing here, Finn?'

Quinn's icy voice cut through the room. She stood in the doorway, wearing her Cheerios hooded sweatshirt over her short practice skirt. Her eyes shot daggers at Rachel. 'I thought you wanted to come to Celibacy Club with me.'

'I did,' Finn said, his face flushing pink. 'I mean, I do.' He glanced at Rachel. How much had Quinn overheard? Suddenly, he was embarrassed that he'd come in here in the first place.

'Let's go, then.' Quinn strode up to Finn and placed her hand calmly on his forearm. He stared at her pale pink fingernails. They looked kind of alien to him. 'I don't want to be late.'

She pulled him toward the door just as Puck stepped in. Quinn crashed into Puck, her head bumping into his chest. They quickly jumped away from each other as if they'd been burned.

'I thought you were catching a ride with Merino?' Finn asked, embarrassed for Puck to see him here as well. Puck was his friend, but if he knew that Finn liked singing, he'd staple a tutu to the quarterback's forehead.

Puck cleared his throat. He'd been following Quinn, hoping for a chance to talk to her again, but now Finn was looking at him suspiciously. Did he have Quinn's lip gloss all over his face or something? To cover, he quickly retorted, 'What are you doing in this dog kennel? Community service?'

Quinn burst into giggles as Rachel pretended to look at a piece of sheet music from her backpack. With her straight blond hair, long eyelashes, and tiny ski-jump nose, Quinn Fabray made Rachel feel like a schnauzer. 'Seriously, Finn.' Quinn's voice was ice. 'What are you doing here?'

'Nothing,' Finn replied, stuffing his hands into the pockets of his jeans. He glanced back at Rachel, giving her an apologetic smile but not saying anything else. 'Let's just go.'

Rachel watched as the three of them disappeared out the door. Her heart sank. Quinn Fabray had absolutely everything, including Finn. Did she really need to insult everyone else, too? And Puck was just a jerk; everyone knew it. He'd punched a kid in the nose just because he was wearing a University of Michigan T-shirt. Normally, insults from the stupid popular kids bounced right off her. After all, when she was a famous Broadway singer, she might get a bad review or two by a clueless critic, and she had to remain unfazed.

She would have taken it all in stride if she hadn't felt as though she and Finn were having…a moment. They really were. She knew it. She hadn't imagined it. Something about him was opening up to her. Maybe Finn was bored with his perfect yet predictable life.

As hurt as she was, she couldn't blame him too much for snubbing her the second his cool friends walked in. Rachel

Berry might be a star-in-waiting, but she was still close to the bottom rung of the McKinley High social ladder. It wasn't Finn's fault if he cared a little too much what his friends thought. He was McKinley High royalty, and while he could afford to spend five minutes talking to Rachel, he couldn't even imagine what the view from the bottom rung was like.

seven

Mercedes's house, Tuesday night

D inner at the Joneses' house was always a noisy affair. Besides Mercedes's immediate family members, there always seemed to be at least one family friend and a couple of her cousins over, too. Mercedes's mom was a firm believer in the old saying 'the more, the merrier.' Her father owned his own dental practice and slapped his wife playfully on the butt when he came in every night, to Mercedes's eternal embarrassment. After everyone else's daily dramas, there was rarely time for Mercedes to talk about her own.

Dinner usually meant a mixture of leftovers, last-minute casseroles with daring combinations of vegetables and cheeses, or takeout from one of the local Chinese, Indian, or pizza restaurants, all of which were on the speed-dial of the Joneses' kitchen phone. That night, it had been deep-dish double-cheese pizza from LaPaloma's, and the guests included two women from her mom's hip-hop aerobics class and Mercedes's second cousin.

It felt good to be back in her room, alone. Her family believed everyone had the right to say something, and so all of them ended up talking at the same time. Her room was quiet and peaceful, with its pale gray walls, chocolate-brown comforter, and thick magenta rug and curtains. Rhinestone-encrusted letters spelling DIVA hung on the wall, above her dresser and next to a brilliant blue lava lamp that Mercedes liked to watch when she was trying to fall asleep. At that moment, though, the only thing that would make her feel better was singing. She stood in front of her full-length mirror and turned to look at herself from different angles. She was what her mother called a 'full-figured girl', and she liked her curves. Most of the time. All the great African-American singers had some booty. Aretha. Ella Fitzgerald. Beyoncé. Mercedes looked over her shoulder at her behind. It was definitely star quality.

She started practicing the Glee song 'Tonight'. But now all she could hear was Rachel's bossy voice drowning out her own – something that was pretty hard to do, since Mercedes had a set of lungs on her. Rachel probably expected to sing lead, as if that weren't Mercedes's God-given right. It was crazy the way Rachel had flounced into practice in her little kindergartener outfit and started critiquing everyone as if she were some kind of expert. In the hour that they practiced, she'd managed to insult everyone's pitch, posture, moves, and outfits. Who the hell did she think she was?

Mercedes glanced at the clock on her computer. It was Tuesday night, and every Tuesday night she and Kurt would text back and forth during *American Idol*, commenting on who sucked and who rocked. It was a tradition dating back to eighth grade, when the music teacher had the two of them sing 'I'll Be There for You' at their graduation ceremony. She loved Kurt for being catty and critical and making her laugh so hard she almost peed her pants. And she felt that Kurt understood her in a way no one else did. Mercedes dreamed about someone fancy signing her to some ginormous record deal, big enough to get her out of Lima, out of Ohio, and out of her boring life. She had star potential, and he knew it.

But Kurt was the one who had brought Rachel to Glee in the first place – as if he didn't have enough faith in Mercedes's ability to bring them together. It was downright insulting. The nerve of him, bringing in a stranger without even thinking to ask anyone else about it.

There was a knock on her door. 'Baby girl,' her mom called, 'you have a visitor.'

Mercedes narrowed her eyes. She didn't get visitors. She didn't really have many friends, and none of them were the type to drop by unannounced. Tina lived on the other side of town, and her mom worked nights, so there was no way she could have gotten to the Joneses' house, and Artie was usually studying on a school night. That left one. She flung open the door.

It was Kurt. Standing in her house, in his pale blue button-down, a snug-fit cashmere V-neck, and navy cashmere socks with yellow toes. Her mother made everyone leave their shoes at the door since having new Brazilian cherry floors installed last summer. Kurt was always so fastidious that the sight of him in stocking feet made Mercedes want to giggle.

Then she remembered Rachel. 'Nice socks,' she said pointedly, planting her hand firmly on her hip and giving him a glare. She wished she was wearing something less schlumpy than her fuchsia velour tracksuit. 'But I don't remember inviting you over. Not that *that* would stop you.'

Kurt brushed his hair off his forehead. 'Cute picture of you in the Mickey Mouse ears, by the way.' He pointed to the wall of photographs in the hallway. 'Is that Cinderella with you?'

'Sleeping Beauty.' Mercedes cleared her throat. 'Seriously, though, if you haven't come to apologize, you can back yourself right out that front door.'

Kurt sighed and fidgeted with the metal clips on his jacket. Mercedes thought it looked like part of a marching-band uniform, yet he insisted it was vintage. 'May I come in? Otherwise I might get roped into performing hip-hop moves with those ladies downstairs.'

'Fine. Come in.' Mercedes stepped back to let him into her room.

'Nice color palette.' Kurt gazed around the room in approval. He'd been at Mercedes's house for pizza a couple of times after mall trips to try out expensive clothes at Bloomingdale's, but he'd never been in her room before. 'Very sophisticated yet fun. And little touches of the diva extraordinaire.' He ran his fingers over a framed photograph of Madonna and gave it a slight bow.

'The apology?' Mercedes refused to back down. Kurt needed to know how insulting it was to have Rachel come in and stomp all over everyone like that. All over *her*.

'Look, I'm sorry if inviting Rachel to Glee Club hurt your feelings, but I'm tired of us getting laughed at all the time.' He fingered the brown fringe on Mercedes's bedside lamp. 'We're good performers, especially you. You're *amazing*. But we haven't really had the chance to come together. And I feel like Rachel can do that.'

Mercedes's cheeks flushed. Okay, it was sweet of him to call her amazing, even though it was just the truth. 'You really think Miss Pink Kneesocks is going to make that much of a difference?' She might not agree with him, but she always respected Kurt's opinion. He had totally called the Adam Lambert thing.

'I swear I do.' Kurt glanced at his watch. He sat down on the edge of Mercedes's bed, sinking slightly into the soft mattress.

'I guess you can consider your apology accepted, then.'

'What does the poster signify?' Kurt was staring at the giant poster of a roaring tiger that stretched over Mercedes's white iMac.

Mercedes smiled sweetly. 'It reminds me that life is a jungle, and if you don't defend yourself, someone bigger than you is just going to take you down.'

'So you're an optimist,' Kurt said, nodding thoughtfully. 'I wouldn't have guessed.'

Mercedes laughed. She loved Kurt – he was her boy – but lately she'd been thinking about him a little differently. He was opinionated and confident, and he always managed to compliment her on something – her new gold hoops, her color of lip gloss – each day. Maybe…

Before she could finish the thought, Kurt spoke up. 'Listen, do you want to get milk shakes or something?' He tossed his head, but his hair, neatly styled, didn't move. 'My dad caught me watching the Style Network's makeover marathon – and it did *not* go over well.'

Mercedes giggled. Kurt's dad had his own car repair shop, and he was the kind of manly man who liked to take apart engines for kicks and didn't get anything that involved singing, dancing, or fashion, Kurt's passions. 'How did you manage to get out?'

Kurt laughed and grabbed a platinum-framed photograph from Mercedes's desk – it was the two of them singing at eighth-grade graduation. 'I can't believe you have this on display. I look like Macaulay Culkin here.' He set down the picture. 'I told him I had a date…with a girl.' His dad had been unreasonably excited by the idea, so much so that Kurt had felt a little bad lying to him. His dad meant well, and deep inside, if he really thought of all the times Kurt had asked for dress-up clothes and Pottery Barn tea sets instead of trucks, he probably knew that Kurt was not interested in girls as anything other than singing partners. But still, he had lent Kurt the keys to his SUV and told him not to stay out too late.

'I can always go for a milk shake,' Mercedes answered. 'Let me change first.' She expected Kurt to leave the room, but instead he just turned his back to Mercedes and examined the clippings stapled to the corkboard next to her door.

'I love how you've saved all of these,' Kurt said, touching the concert ticket stubs that filled the board. Some of them had papers with autographs on them.

Mercedes slipped out of her velour pants and into a pair of jeans. Why wouldn't Kurt just leave the room? Did he...like her? She started putting the pieces together. Coming over to her house unannounced to apologize? Inviting her out for milk shakes? Not leaving the room while she was getting changed? What other explanation could there possibly be?

For the first time since Rachel Berry had stepped into the Glee practice room, Mercedes started to feel a teeny bit better.

eight

Lima Freeze, Tuesday night

The Lima Freeze, in addition to the Lima Galleria Cineplex 8, the Olive Garden at the mall, and the benches at the entrance of the nature trail in MacArthur City Park, was one of the few, and consequently the most popular, of the Lima date night venues. It had been a Friendly's ice cream parlor that folded years ago and was bought by a local couple and slightly improved. The Freeze was located along a strip of Route 17 between the farms at the outskirts of Lima and the downtown area, which had several historic buildings in various states of disrepair. Along the way, Mercedes watched as they passed the Wegmans, the local grocery chain, a karate place, a Pizza Hut, the senior citizens' center, three banks, and a handful of other businesses that always appeared to be on the brink of going under. Kurt had cranked the stereo, which was hooked into his iPod, and Kanye West was thumping through the car speakers.

'I could get used to these darkened windows.' Mercedes touched up her curly hair in the sun visor mirror. 'I feel like a rock star.'

'Someday, my dear.' Kurt pulled into the parking lot. Nearly all the spots were taken by minivans or beat-up Buicks. Families with squirming kids were ordering from the take-out window and sitting at the sticky wooden picnic tables on the little concrete patio outside. Through the slightly fogged-up windows, the booths all looked filled.

'Damn the masses.' Kurt thumped his fist against the steering wheel in mock anger as he pulled in next to a shiny BMW. 'They had the same brilliant idea we did.'

Mercedes didn't mind the crowd. She liked the idea of being seen on a date with Kurt. She even liked just riding around with him in his dad's SUV. It felt good to drive through the streets of Lima perched so high, looking through tinted-glass windows at the town she'd lived in her whole life. It seemed much prettier. 'Let's go. I'm dying for my sugar rush.'

Inside, the Lima Freeze was packed, and the windows were fogged with the warmth of so many bodies. Kurt glanced around for any of the football players who harassed him, but he didn't see any. A lucky break. It was bad enough to be slushied at school, but the last thing he needed was a milk shake thrown in his face in public. He had a hard time explaining to his father why so many of his shirts came home stained blue and purple and red.

'I'll have a Death by Chocolate frappe, please,' Mercedes told the bored-looking teen behind the counter. 'Extra thick.'

'A hot fudge sundae. Whipped cream. Don't forget the cherry.' Kurt eyed the group of soccer boys in a corner booth. One of them got up to refill his water glass, and Kurt watched as his calves flexed with each step.

As they scanned the ice cream parlor in vain for a table, the door opened and in walked Finn Hudson with Quinn Fabray, still in her Cheerios practice hoodie, on his arm. 'Barbie and Ken just showed up,' Mercedes announced.

'Mmm.' Kurt eyed the couple, trying to ignore the patter of his heart at the sight of Finn Hudson. 'Looks like the Celibacy Club got out early.'

'That table over there's going to open up. Let's move over.' Mercedes grabbed Kurt's sleeve and tugged him aside. She stared at the three girls who were slurping the last of their milk shakes through straws. Table service was first come, first served; at rush hour, that meant you had to be ready to pounce.

Finn and Quinn got to the front counter.

'She's cute, but did you ever notice how her ears are kind of pointy, like an elf's?' Kurt whispered in Mercedes's ear. She giggled. She hadn't noticed, but now that Kurt had pointed them out, she could totally picture Quinn running around with a quiver of arrows in those *Lord of the Rings* movies.

71

'Excuse me,' Quinn muttered, casually letting her purse bump into Kurt's back so that he'd take a step away. She liked coming to the Lima Freeze, but it was always so overrun by losers. 'Finn, I'll take a root beer float, with frozen yogurt and diet root beer.' She smoothed the sides of her practice skirt. Usually she was careful about the number of calories she took in every day, but what with her good genes – her mother was still a size four – and her Cheerios workout, she figured she deserved a treat. But she knew not to go too crazy or she'd be sluggish on her flips. 'I'll find a table. Those girls are almost done.'

'I'm sorry. We're actually waiting for that table.' Kurt handed the girl at the counter a crisp ten-dollar bill.

Quinn stared at Kurt as if he were a cockroach. 'I didn't see your name on it.' She spun on the heel of her cheerleading sneakers, and her blond ponytail whirled through the air behind her. He and Mercedes watched as Quinn sashayed up to the table where the three girls were sitting, still sipping from their milk shakes. They watched in awe as Quinn said a few words to the girls, who quickly stuffed their napkins into their almost-empty glasses and scooted out of the booth happily, with smiles on their faces.

Quinn slipped into the booth, wiped the table with a napkin, and then waved at Finn, pointedly looking past Kurt and Mercedes.

'Oh no, she didn't.' Mercedes wiped a trickle of ice cream off the rim of her milk shake glass. She glanced around the crowded restaurant. None of the other people looked even remotely interested in giving up their seats.

'I'm, uh, sorry about that.' Finn glanced nervously over his shoulder at Quinn, who was already leaning back in the booth talking to the soccer guys sitting behind her. A tiny strip of skin showed as her shirt crawled up her perfectly flat stomach. 'Were you waiting for that table?'

Kurt's mouth opened, but no words came out. Finn. Hudson. Was talking to him. Sure, he wasn't the sharpest knife in the drawer, but Kurt wasn't interested in his mind. Finn was gorgeous. He was the only guy on the football team who always offered to hold Kurt's designer jacket before the players slammed Kurt into the Dumpster. Besides that, Finn's hair was always perfectly mussed. His cheekbones looked like they could cut ice, and his brown eyes were like the pools of chocolate in *Charlie and the Chocolate Factory*. Kurt had admired him from afar since that day freshman year when Puck Puckerman and Jack Kurpatwinski had tried to throw Kurt into a vat of grease in the cafeteria kitchen after fried-chicken day. Finn told them to knock it off, and they did. He was like Superman.

'Yeah, we were,' Mercedes answered as she kicked Kurt in the foot. Why was he acting like such a tool in front of Finn Hudson? Just because Finn was popular didn't mean Kurt had to act like such a moron. It reminded her of their family's golden retriever, who would flop down on the ground and roll around on her back whenever a bigger dog showed up – 'classic submissive behavior', her dad said. Kurt wasn't exactly on his back but, man, he could show a little more backbone. 'Don't worry about it. We'll just stand here at the counter. Who needs a seat?' Mercedes said with a fake smile.

'Cool.' Finn ordered two root beer floats, missing the irony in Mercedes's voice. As he waited for the floats, he looked around the place and then turned back to Kurt and Mercedes. 'Aren't you two in that singing club?'

Mercedes and Kurt shared a glance. Kurt still couldn't talk. How was it possible that Finn Hudson knew something – anything – about him? Mercedes had to answer. 'Yup, we are.' She sipped her milk shake. 'What's it to you?'

Finn stared at his shoes. He was grateful when the counter girl handed him his two root beer floats. It gave him something else to look at. He was a little embarrassed that he'd been so moved by Rachel's performance after school. 'I, uh, saw Rachel. Singing after school. She said you were going to perform. At the recital.'

Oh my God, Kurt thought. It was so adorable how Finn couldn't speak in complete sentences. 'Friday,' Kurt managed to croak out.

Finn smiled at them. Even Mercedes felt her knees weaken. It felt good to have a popular, gorgeous jock talking to them like they were human beings. 'Well, good luck,' Finn said. 'I'd better, uh, get going with these.'

'Finn.' Quinn ran her tube of lip gloss across her lips and opened and closed them several times to distribute the gloss evenly. She watched as Finn placed the diet root beer float on the table in front of her. 'What were you doing over there?'

'What? Oh.' Finn slid into the booth. One of the defensive ends walked by and held out his hand for a high five. Finn slapped it. 'I was just talking to those guys.' He pulled the wrapper off his straw and stuck it into the float.

'I saw that.' Quinn took a tiny sip of her float. Had he remembered to get frozen yogurt? And diet root beer? It tasted awfully sweet. And Quinn hadn't got a body like hers eating full-fat ice cream. 'But why were you wasting your time talking to them? They're, like, a thousand miles beneath you.'

Finn slurped his float. Quinn could be so...harsh. 'I was just being friendly.'

'Well, you should save it.' Quinn took another sip of her float and then pushed it away. She could practically feel her skirt waistband getting tighter. She was certain that Finn had messed up her order because he'd been too busy talking to that gay guy and that girl who had no business ordering a milk shake. 'Some of the Cheerios are planning a prank at the fall music recital on Friday. Something to really embarrass that Rachel girl.'

'What?' Finn almost choked on his float. 'Why would you want to do that?' Was it because Finn had been talking to Rachel in the auditorium? Quinn couldn't tell he was attracted to Rachel, could she? Suddenly, Finn thought of that creepy old movie where the crazy girlfriend throws the guy's bunny into a pot of boiling water.

75

'Do you really need to ask?' Quinn tapped her spoon against the sticky table. 'It was humiliating how that crazy nobody ranted about the Cheerios' voting booth on the morning announcements. In front of the entire school.' She rubbed her lips together again. 'She definitely has to pay.'

'I don't know.' Finn wiped his mouth with the back of his hand. 'It doesn't seem like that big a deal. She was just expressing her opinion, right?'

'What gave her the right to do that?' Quinn crossed her arms. 'What would happen if we let her get away with it? There'd be total social revolt if all the losers could talk about us like that.' Quinn could tell Finn was unconvinced. She bit her lip. She was losing him, and she didn't even really have him yet. She never would have had to work this hard to get Puck on her side. He would have done whatever she wanted, without her having to beg.

If she wanted Finn, though, she didn't want him to be halfheartedly hers. She needed his full cooperation in this relationship, or they wouldn't become the resident It couple. She reached out and put her hand on Finn's. He dropped his spoon, but she didn't take her hand away. 'Some of the football players are coming, too.' She fluttered her long lashes at him. 'Are you in? Or are you out?'

Finn stared at her perfect pink fingernails. They were so smooth and straight. He imagined those perfect hands on his shoulders as they slow danced at the homecoming dance. If he wanted to go with Quinn, he couldn't fight her on this.

He didn't think Rachel was so bad. Even though she'd sounded kind of crazy ranting on the PA, wasn't she right? And even if she wasn't, she was kind of nice and didn't deserve to be humiliated.

Quinn tapped her fingers against Finn's hand, prompting him. Even though he didn't know her that well yet, he could tell she was the kind of girl who was used to getting what she wanted. If Finn couldn't give that to her, some other guy would be more than happy to.

'Okay,' he heard himself say in a voice that didn't sound like his own. 'What do you need me to do?'

nine

Choir room, Wednesday morning

On Wednesday morning, Rachel demanded that the Glee kids get passes out of their study halls to come to the choir room for an extra practice session. For half an hour, they crowded around the piano singing 'Tonight' and trying to do the steps she'd storyboarded for them last night while watching the movie version of *West Side Story* for inspiration. They had run through the routine half a dozen times before Artie wheeled over to the side of the room.

'What are you doing?' Rachel demanded. She had on a white puff-sleeved button-down under a wool herringbone jumper, but she still managed to move with as much energy as a professional dancer, or at least a Cheerio during one of

Coach Sylvester's 'elimination' practices. 'We haven't nailed the footwork yet.'

'You don't want to see me dehydrate.' Artie pulled a bottle of water from his backpack and took a swig. 'It's not pretty.'

'I'm with Artie. I think we could all use a break,' Mercedes admitted, throwing herself down on one of the plastic chairs. 'My bones are not used to working this hard.'

'I'm starting to work up a sweat.' Kurt touched the back of his hand to his forehead. 'And I can't pull off the sweaty look.' He grabbed a folder and fanned his face.

'Y-y-yeah, Rachel,' Tina said. 'We're tired. Plus, I've got homework to do for tomorrow.'

Rachel clenched her fists at her sides in frustration. Two days. They had only two days to perfect their routine, and it wasn't there yet. They were good, but not great. If they wanted to impress the whole school, they didn't have time for paltry things like water breaks. She'd heard that when Madonna was getting ready to go on tour, she'd practice for eighteen hours straight without even taking a pee break.

Still, Artie was in a wheelchair. Maybe she needed to give him a break. But was it too much to ask that the rest of them – with two working legs – work a little harder? *Pick your battles*, she thought. She sighed and sat down on the piano bench. 'Five minutes.'

Mercedes leaned back in her chair. 'I'm not going to practice,' she sang, improvising. 'I said no, no, no.' The others, except Rachel, laughed.

'Have you all seen the Lady Gaga video for "Just Dance"? I love it.' Tina took a sip from her Diet Coke bottle.

'She's Eurotrashtastic in that. It looks like an American Apparel commercial.' Kurt loved American Apparel, but the closest one was in Dayton, an hour's drive away. He went there once a month to stock up on tight-fitting T-shirts, knee-length cardigans, and whatever came in turquoise.

Tina sang a few lines from the song, her platform Mary Janes sliding across the linoleum tiles. Her black-and-red plaid skirt, the flaps held together by five giant metal safety pins, flared out as she moved.

'Damn, girl.' Mercedes started humming the backup part. 'You're feeling the Lady Gaga today.'

'*What's goin' on, on the floor?*'

'Tina, what else have you been hiding from us?' Kurt raised his eyebrows as everyone watched her in amazement.

Rachel rolled her eyes. Sure, she was happy Tina was coming out of her shell. Maybe singing would give her enough confidence to overcome her stutter. But that didn't mean Rachel wanted to see Tina steal the show away from her.

'You should save those moves for next Friday night,' Rachel blurted out. 'You don't want to use them all up on us now.'

The others exchanged glances. 'What's next Friday night?' Artie asked cautiously.

'Um, just the homecoming dance?' Rachel's eyes widened. 'We can all celebrate our dazzling recital performance at the dance next week.'

'How would we do that if we're not th-th-there?' Tina flopped down into one of the plastic chairs and took a giant sip of water. Rachel breathed a sigh of relief. She didn't agree with the Andy Warhol saying that everyone gets fifteen minutes of fame. It was a little too egalitarian. She'd prefer it to be based on ability instead.

'You're not going?' Rachel had always dreamed about going to high school dances. She'd had a closet full of play clothes when she was growing up, and her dads would help her transform the dining room into a ballroom.

'Hell to the no,' Mercedes said, staring down at the piano. She would have liked to go, but only with Kurt, and if he was going to ask her, he probably would have done it by now. She glanced at him. He was adjusting his hair.

'I'm not really equipped for dancing in large crowds of people.' Artie rolled back on his wheels. The only person he could imagine going with was Tina, and it would probably be embarrassing for her to be the only one with a date who had wheels.

'I get n-n-nervous in crowds.' Tina fiddled with the black leather cuff bracelet on her left wrist.

'None of you are going?' Rachel couldn't believe it. 'The homecoming dance is one of the seminal events of any student's high school career. Kurt?'

'I've considered it.' Kurt touched his hair. He was wearing his favorite Marc Jacobs button-down and the only pair of jeans he would wear, his Rock & Republic dark-wash skinny

82

jeans. 'I just bought an awesome new Tom Ford suit on eBay, and it would be the only place I could wear it.'

Rachel clapped her hands. 'Yes! Let's all go, then.' She found it disturbing that Kurt knew so much about fashion.

'I just said I'd considered it.' Kurt glared at Rachel. Must she always be so peppy? 'But I don't really want to deal with the popular kids. They'll be out in full force, probably drunk and ready to terrorize.' He smoothed his shirt. 'It's a really great suit. I don't know if I can risk it.'

'This is shameful, everyone!' Rachel slapped her hand down on the piano. She felt as angry as she had after seeing the Cheerios charging students to vote. 'Why should the *jocks* be the only ones who are allowed to participate in McKinley High's activities? They've already got most of the funding for their sports and clubs, and they get away with throwing slushies in everyone's face. We can't take it lying down.'

Artie straightened his tie. 'That's because they're the beautiful people.' Although Tina was prettier than anyone else in school, in Artie's opinion. The blue streaks she'd put in a few weeks ago were like ribbons in her long, shiny black locks. He even liked the crazy eye makeup she wore – bright pinks or bright blues in electric cotton candy colors. And she was a nice person, which was priceless. 'Beautiful people historically have been able to get away with anything.'

Rachel threw her hands up in the air. 'That doesn't make it right!' She turned to Tina, sensing a potential ally. 'Tina, you're a great dancer. Wouldn't it be fun for you to get all dressed up in a...' She stared at Tina's Goth outfit. 'In a...fancy black dress and some new spiked leather bracelets? And step out on the dance floor and show people how to do it?'

Tina shook her head. 'I-I-I don't think so.' She stared at the floor. 'I can dance in front of y-y-you guys, but not the whole school. Someone would probably trip me, just to see how I landed.'

'You guys.' Rachel stepped back. This was shocking. 'We *have* to go. We have to show the rest of the school that we won't be pushed around or influenced by what everyone else thinks.' Last spring, Rachel stayed home from the Under the Sea end-of-the-year dance, pretending that she was busy working on her MySpace page. But really she was too embarrassed after the school president fiasco to face the student body. She wasn't going to let that happen again this year. Date or no date, she wanted to go to the homecoming dance.

Kurt sighed. While he admired Rachel's change-the-world spirit, it also just made him tired. 'That's all very nice and good in theory, but it's just not practical. The rest of the school *does* push us around, and everyone *is* influenced by what they think.'

'I'm with Kurt.' Mercedes looked sad. 'What's the point of going and calling more attention to ourselves? I'm not exactly hard to miss – I'm one of ten black kids at this school, and I'm not exactly a toothpick.'

Artie and Tina were nodding in agreement. Rachel wanted

to pull out her hair. She couldn't believe they were all giving up without a fight. Had they never seen a Broadway musical? Didn't they know that you had to never give up? Always keep fighting? It was even more frustrating because she could tell they *wanted* to go – she could read it all over their faces – but they were too terrified. Why? Because some of the popular kids would make fun of them?

Rachel stared at the clock above the door, wishing it were time to move on to the next class. The choir room felt stifling all of a sudden. If the Glee kids were this timid, maybe she shouldn't be putting all her eggs in the Glee basket.

What she needed was a plan B.

ten

Miss Pillsbury's guidance office, later on Wednesday

Miss Pillsbury had been the guidance counselor at McKinley High for only a year and a half, but she was a vast improvement over Ms Delzer, who'd been forced to resign after a local military recruiter pled guilty to bribing her to encourage particularly athletic students to enlist. She fled the state before charges could be brought against her. Miss Pillsbury was young, with orange-red hair cut in a perky bob, and she didn't walk through the halls with that burned-out look in her eyes that most teachers got after a few years. She had wide eyes that made her look like a Precious Moments figurine.

'Rachel, what can I help you with today?' Miss Pillsbury smiled sweetly and crossed her hands on her unnaturally neat desk. Behind her, her computer monitor showed a screensaver of inspirational phrases flashing through black space. Rachel read YOU CAN DO IT and HOLD FAST TO YOUR DREAMS and THE WORLD IS YOUR OYSTER: GO AHEAD AND EAT IT before she had to look away. A large potted tree loomed in the corner of the room, its fronds reaching toward the sun. Shelves of study guides and college catalogs lined the built-in bookshelves, though Rachel suspected that most of them had never been touched. McKinley High students were not an ambitious bunch.

Rachel wiped her feet on the WELCOME mat inside the door. Even though they were indoors. Rachel had heard that Miss Pillsbury had a thing about dirt. 'I am in serious need of guidance.'

'You came to the right place.' Miss Pillsbury, in her kelly green blouse with a giant bow at her neck, looked like she should be going door-to-door selling Girl Scout cookies. 'Have a seat.'

Rachel glanced over her shoulder as she sank into the vinyl armchair opposite Miss Pillsbury's desk. One glass wall of the guidance counselor's office looked out on the main hallway, and Rachel kept getting the creepy sensation that someone was making puckered-lip fish faces against the glass behind her head. 'I think I've gone as far as I can go at McKinley High.'

Miss Pillsbury blinked. Her voice was like a glass of warm milk. 'Okay, Rachel. Tell me why you think that. Are you not being challenged?'

'I've read online about performing arts high schools – like in *Fame*? – and I just feel like I might be a better fit at a place like that.' She imagined the perfect schedule – vocal training, aerobics, tap dance, dramatic arts, lunch.

Miss Pillsbury nodded noncommittally. She occasionally had gifted students come to her about their fears of not realizing their potential, but far more often she found herself talking to students who had no interest in realizing their potential. Rachel Berry was an interesting case. She was one of those students whom teachers either loved or hated; although she got excellent grades and participated in class with a zeal that most students could only muster for lunch, her personality was a little...abrasive. 'Are you having a hard time fitting in at McKinley?'

'What? No.' Rachel raised her nose in the air. 'I mean, I don't care about fitting in. That's not what this is about.'

Miss Pillsbury nodded her head slowly. She never saw Rachel talking to friends or hanging out with groups of people in the cafeteria. Not that Miss Pillsbury could blame her for that. The cafeteria was one of the filthiest places in the entire school. A kitchen sink housed more germs than the handle of a toilet, she had read, and she was pretty sure the sinks in the cafeteria were not immaculate. Suddenly, she felt a little woozy. She quickly squirted some of her liquid hand sanitizer into her palms, letting the lemony smell waft its way into her nostrils. It had a calming effect. 'What is it about, then?' She was used to asking students series of questions, trying to get the teens to figure out what they wanted out of life and why they were here.

Rachel took a deep breath and stared at the rack of self-help pamphlets behind the desk. Miss Pillsbury wasn't listening at all, which didn't seem like an excellent trait for a guidance counselor. Rachel spoke in a calm voice. 'It only makes sense that someone of my caliber and talents receive the training to match.'

Miss Pillsbury rubbed her temples with the tips of her clear-polished nails, trying to tell herself that if only all her students were this ambitious, her job would be much easier. 'Yes, I can see your point.'

'Good.' Rachel beamed.

But Miss Pillsbury had heard about Rachel Berry's tendencies to overreact. The counselor tried to keep an empathetic look on her face. 'Rachel, I know you are a very talented young lady. I heard you sing during the announcements, and I think you were quite lovely.' Which was true, although when Rachel was singing this morning, all Miss Pillsbury could think about was how unsanitary the microphones must be, with multiple people using them. They had to be hotbeds of spittle and germs.

'Thank you.' Rachel nodded. She sensed Miss Pillsbury's hesitation, but as a school administrator, wasn't she obligated to attempt to satisfy the needs of her students?

'I could certainly look into performing arts schools for you, do a little digging around. But are you sure you've exhausted the creative outlets McKinley has to offer? There's jazz band, and the school musical coming up this fall. Oh, and Glee Club.' Looking over Rachel's shoulder, Miss Pillsbury spotted a thumbprint on the glass wall. Her hands itched to grab her bottle of Windex. 'I hear they're looking for new members.'

Rachel sank back in her chair. 'I know about Glee Club. They specially requested that I join and give them help, so I did it.' She shrugged. Her crisp pale pink polo shirt with the puff sleeves was still unsullied by slushies today, and she was hoping to keep it up. 'But they just don't take it seriously. Plus, Mr Ryerson hardly counts as a trained vocal coach. He isn't even there for practices.'

'How long have you been a member?'

Rachel stiffened. 'Since Monday.' Her voice was defensive.

Miss Pillsbury nodded, as if this were a somewhat reasonable amount of time. 'Well, maybe what they need is someone like you to help them take it seriously.' Miss Pillsbury caught a glimpse of Will Schuester out in the hallway, handing a paper back to a student who had a scowl on her face. 'Why don't you give it a couple more weeks with Glee and see how it goes? It seems awfully early in the school year to be making such large life decisions.'

'I just feel like the clock is ticking on me. . . . I won't be this young and trainable forever.'

'I know.' Mr Schuester was still talking to the girl, and Miss Pillsbury hoped that if she timed it right, she could leave her office right when he was finished and they could walk to the teachers' lunchroom together. She grabbed the Tupperware container of triple-washed chopped carrots and lettuce on the corner of her desk and stood up. 'But there's a lot to offer here, and a student with your talent can really make a difference and stand out.'

'I guess you're right.' Rachel got to her feet. Her one reservation about attending a specialty performing arts school was that she would just be one of many, many talented students. Maybe she wanted to stay in the small pond, where she could pretty much be the biggest fish imaginable. 'I'll stick with Glee for a while, at least. Maybe I can turn the group around. Thank you for the encouragement.'

'Anytime, Rachel.' Miss Pillsbury hoped the girl wouldn't take that literally. She got the feeling that Rachel would use her as a therapist if she could. She walked Rachel to the door and grabbed her purse from the coat tree in the corner. 'Good luck with Glee.'

Rachel felt better as she walked out of the office. That was, until she saw that the giant banner that stretched over the main trophy case announcing the Fall in Love with Music recital on Friday had been completely desecrated. MUSIC had been crossed out, and A PILE OF POOP had been written above it. Students were nudging each other and laughing as they passed it, and Rachel felt her cheeks flush with anger. Maybe she could be good for McKinley High, but it clearly wasn't good enough for her.

'On second thought, Miss Pillsbury, I would still like the

information on the performing arts schools. Just to keep my options open.' She flounced down the hallway to her locker.

'What was that all about?' Mr Schuester stared down the hall after the pouting girl, who looked vaguely familiar to him. He'd been trying to explain to a sophomore why she had failed his Spanish exam, but just as she walked away he managed to overhear the end of Miss Pillsbury's conversation. 'Is someone looking into performing arts schools?'

Miss Pillsbury locked the door to her office. Even though she was anywhere from well liked to easily ignored by the students, she had a paralyzing fear that some of them would sneak into her office when she wasn't there and do something vile on her carpet. 'Yes. Do you know Rachel Berry?' she whispered to Will. Although she generally didn't discuss students with other teachers, Will didn't count, as he was her lunch buddy.

'Sure, she was in my class last year,' he said. 'Now she's singing on the morning announcements, right?'

'Exactly.' She shook her head as she caught sight of the desecrated banner. 'I'm going to have to call a janitor to take that down.' She couldn't even look at it.

'Rachel is really looking to transfer to another school, with better music programs?' Mr Schuester slung his leather messenger bag across his shoulder. 'That's such a shame. She can really sing.'

The two of them walked through the quiet hallways to the faculty lunchroom. 'It is a shame.' Miss Pillsbury paused in front of the trophy case. 'I know McKinley has a rich Glee history.'

'Exactly. See those trophies? When I went here, we won sectionals every year, and we even won regionals. Once.' He stared at the shiny brass statuette of a figure singing into a microphone. 'We had so many kids trying out for Glee that we had alternates, and second alternates.' He glanced at Miss Pillsbury. 'We ruled the school. You should have seen us.'

'I would have liked to,' Miss Pillsbury said softly, wondering what Will looked like as a teenager. Probably just skinnier, with the same mop of curly hair.

Mr Schuester turned his head, and his eyes rested on a Cheerios trophy. One, two, ten, fifteen Cheerios trophies, all with brass girls raising pom-poms. There was nothing wrong with physical abilities, Mr Schuester thought. But the school used to be able to cater to more students than just the physically gifted ones. Things had really gone downhill since his days as a student, when someone with musical talents was just as admired as someone who could toss a football, or throw a fat pitch down the middle of the plate, or execute the perfect round-off.

It kind of broke his heart.

eleven

McKinley High hallway, Thursday morning

'**C**an I copy your English homework? I forgot to do it.' Brittany pulled her long blond hair back into a high ponytail as she walked down the hallway with Santana and Quinn. Her Cheerios uniform showed off her long, slender legs.

'Brit, the assignment was an essay on "How I Spent My Summer Vacation".' Santana pulled a lip gloss from her hobo purse and smeared some on her lips. 'I think Mr Horn would know that you didn't go to Nicaragua to visit your granny Maria.'

'Shoot.' Brittany's face fell. 'What did *you* do this summer, Quinn?'

Quinn rolled her eyes. Although Brittany and Santana were allegedly her best friends, she was always surprised that Brittany managed to function as well as she did, considering her nearly nonexistent IQ. Quinn would much rather just enjoy the walks from class to class with her friends than listen to Brittany's inane questions. Everyone knew who they were. And everyone always stared at them, in the good, envious way, not the broccoli-in-your-teeth way.

As she was formulating a clever response to Brittany, she felt her backpack vibrate. Quickly, she dug through it for her iPhone, a back-to-school present from her doting father. It was a text. She didn't recognize the number, but when she clicked on it, she knew right away who it was from. She could practically hear the challenge in Puck's flirtatious voice. *Bail on yr girlfriends and meet me in the janitor's closet by the libe. It's not under the bleachers, but gotta see u.*

Quinn's heart thumped so loudly she was sure Brittany and Santana could hear it. Although the two of them were her closest friends, they couldn't, under any circumstances, find out about her and Puck. Santana for obvious reasons – she was jealous enough of Quinn as it was, but if she found out that Quinn was hooking up with the guy she was after, there would be serious trouble. And Brittany was simply too dumb to be relied on to keep any secret. She meant well, but her brain cells were seriously defective. 'It's from Finn,' Quinn lied. 'He is such a sweetheart.'

'Awww,' Brittany and Santana cried in unison. A group of

freshman girls jumped out of their way. One of the advantages of being a Cheerio was that you could walk straight down the middle of the hallway, and people would move to accommodate you. 'That is so cute.'

'You guys really are the perfect couple.' Santana held out her hand to high-five a fellow Cheerio as she passed. 'I can't believe it took so long for you to get together.'

'Like Cinderella and Prince…Prince…William.' Brittany smiled.

'Prince Charming,' Santana corrected her.

Quinn fought the urge to roll her eyes again. (Her mother always reminded her that eye-rolling caused crow's-feet later in life.) Everyone kept saying the exact same thing to her, as if she and Finn had been made only for each other. She wasn't sure she believed that. Besides, it sucked all the romance out of it.

It wasn't like with Puck, whom she clearly wasn't supposed to be with. He was totally wrong for her. Everyone knew that he'd slept with all kinds of MILFs through his joke of a pool-cleaning business over the summer, and although he'd gone to the last meeting of the Celibacy Club, she seriously doubted his commitment.

Which made him all the more exciting.

'There is a serious lack of eligible guys of quality in this godforsaken high school. I don't know why it took me so long to find him, either.' Quinn tried to put away her phone without answering it.

'Puck's hot,' Brittany said. 'And that guy in math class who always sits at the front of the room and wears sweaters.'

'That's Mr DeWitt.' Santana scowled at her. 'The teacher? Remember?'

Quinn gave up. She stared at Puck's text one more time before writing back. *I can't meet you. I have to go to class.* Her thumb paused. *And this thing between us cannot go on.* The girls passed a classroom with an open window, and the smell of freshly cut grass wafted through the halls, bringing Quinn back to the other afternoon, under the bleachers. It had to end with Puck just so she could stop this craziness.

Almost immediately, her phone vibrated again. *I just want to talk. Please.*

It was the *please* that did it for her. It made Puck's request sound so simple, and she felt that she would be unreasonable to say no. He just wanted to talk. That was only fair. They would stand there in the dark janitor's closet and mutually agree that while there was some level of physical attraction between the two of them, it didn't make sense for them to pursue it. Quinn would admit to herself that she had only submitted to the attraction in a period of moral weakness during which she had briefly forgotten her way, and she would ask God to forgive her brief indiscretion.

Fine, she texted back before throwing her phone into her bag.

'I just remembered – I've got to return a book to the library.' The words sounded like a blatant lie coming out of Quinn's mouth – but Santana and Brittany were arguing about which had more calories, a carrot or a celery stick, and they just nodded their heads at Quinn. 'And I've got to go to the restroom, too, so don't wait for me.'

''Kay. See you in class.' Santana waved over her shoulder as Quinn turned to go up the stairwell to the library.

As Quinn climbed the stairs, she tried to compose her thoughts. She was just going to be honest with Puck – or sort of honest with him. She would tell him that she liked him but they didn't have a future. She wouldn't mention the fact that her knees got weak when she thought about the way he touched the back of her neck as he kissed her, or that the smell of grass was now something she associated only with him.

The upstairs hallway was nearly empty as students hurried to class. Quinn glanced at the library, almost wishing she actually had a library book to return so that she hadn't lied. It was never good to lie, as lies always caught up with you in the end. She spotted the janitor's closet; its dark green unmarked door blended in with the tile walls of the hall. The closet was conveniently located next to the girls' bathroom – anyone who saw her might think she was headed to powder her nose. Quinn took a deep breath, feeling the way she did whenever she stood at the top of the Cheerios' pyramid – on the narrow line between exhilaration and disaster.

She opened the door.

twelve

Janitor's closet, Thursday morning

Puck was leaning against the wall of the janitor's closet in the dark, waiting for Quinn. He flipped open his phone to check the time. A tiny part of him worried she wouldn't come. What if she'd just said she would come to get him to leave her alone, and now she was sitting in her stupid English class, giggling with Santana and Brittany, probably laughing about how Puck was such a fake for pretending to be such a player when he was getting all soft on a girl like Quinn. Here he was, waiting for her in a dark janitor's closet he'd only discovered because he and his buddies had locked some freshman loser in there once. Puck's face burned.

Then a magical thing happened. The door opened, and Quinn Fabray scooted inside. 'Why are you standing here with the light off?' She fumbled around looking for a light switch by the door.

Immediately, Puck's confidence returned. If Quinn Fabray, founder and president of the Celibacy Club, had agreed to meet him in a dark janitor's closet, he was seriously doing something right. 'You don't want anyone to see us, do you?' He grabbed for Quinn's hand and held it in his.

Quinn was quiet as her eyes adjusted to the dark. This was already off to the wrong start. Her church – the Kingdom of His Faith Fellowship – had once sponsored a haunted house and hayride out at Old Miller's Farm. The haunted house consisted of a long tunnel whose walls were made of a black plastic that buckled in the wind. Each person had to go through the tunnel alone, in complete darkness, while creepy music played. Occasionally someone in a sheet would jump out at you. It had been the scariest feeling in the world – not being able to see anything in front of you, even when you knew it was there. Quinn had almost wet her pants the first time someone jumped out at her.

This, somehow, was scarier. She shook Puck's warm hand off hers. The janitor's closet smelled like Lysol and like Puck. Unlike Finn, he didn't wear any cologne, and so his smell, instead, was a mixture of deodorant and some musky scent that could only be his own.

'I knew you'd show up,' Puck said cockily, stepping closer to Quinn. She took a few steps backward until her back was pressed against the closed door. She could barely see his face in the darkness, but she could sense that he was just inches from her. Oh, crap. All her plans flew out the window as her heart thudded against her rib cage.

'And how did you know that?' Quinn started to ask, but before she could finish, Puck's lips were touching hers, gently at first, then with more pressure. And she couldn't help but kiss back. His mouth tasted like chocolate. Quinn was reminded of the double chocolate fudge brownies she used to buy at Auntie Amy's at the mall – melt-in-your-mouth warm and delicious, and completely terrible for you. Puck, in a nutshell.

'You taste so good,' Puck said as his mouth moved to Quinn's neck. 'Like some kind of really delicious citrus fruit.'

'My lip gloss.' Quinn closed her eyes at the feel of his lips at the base of her neck. 'It's mango.'

'Mango,' Puck repeated, his lips mouthing the word against her skin. She shuddered.

Outside, the bell rang, shattering the spell Quinn had fallen under. Quickly, while she could still think, she ran her hands against the wall and found the light switch. She flicked it on, flooding the room with light.

'What did you do that for?' Puck held his hand over his eyes to shield them from the sudden light. Quinn looked so out of place in the dingy janitor's closet, in her perky Cheerios uniform.

'I came here to talk.' Quinn crossed her arms over her chest, blinking to get used to the light. What had she been thinking, coming to a filthy janitor's closet to make out with Puck? She hadn't been thinking, that was the thing. At least not with her brain. In the light, the room was much less exotic and thrilling. A giant metal shelving unit lined one wall, chock full of cans of Lysol, bottles of Windex, and other cleaning materials of various shapes and sizes. In the corner was a giant metal bucket on wheels and a mop that looked as if it had been wiping up filth for fifty years. 'You said you wanted to talk.'

Puck hung his head. 'I know. But just when you walked through that door...' He trailed off, looking up at Quinn with a puppy-dog look that somehow came off as extra devious. 'I couldn't help myself.'

Quinn patted her hair in place. 'Well? What did you want to talk about?' Her eyes landed on a big white bucket with a label that read VOMIT ABSORBENT AND DEODORIZER POWDER. It must be a year's supply of that orangey-pink sawdust the janitor threw on the floor whenever some poor kid upchucked. Not romantic.

'I don't know.' Puck was suddenly shy. 'I thought, maybe, since there's clearly something between us, you'd want to go to the homecoming dance together.'

'What?' She felt a rush of triumph that he wanted to go with her, not Santana. Not anyone else. With her. 'That's really sweet, Puck. But there's no way that could happen.'

Puck stepped back. Was she saying he wasn't good enough for her? He'd raised almost four thousand dollars cleaning pools that summer, and he still had a couple hundred dollars left after all the six-packs and video games he'd bought. Plenty left to buy tickets to the dance, a corsage, and a six-pack of wine coolers for afterward. 'Why not?'

'Get real, Puck.' She shook her head sadly and tried not to think about dancing with him. She'd bet he knew how to move. His body seemed to know how to do a lot of things. 'There's no way we could ever go public as a couple. I have my reputation to think about.'

Puck ran his hand over his Mohawk. 'What the hell does that mean? I've got my reputation to live up to, too.'

'Exactly.' Quinn sighed. 'Your reputation for getting into the pants of every single girl who so much as smiles at you.'

'Hey, don't get mad at me just because the ladies like me.'

Quinn stared at the vomit-absorbent bucket. Puck's cockiness was infuriating but also incredibly sexy. Puck was famous for going through girls like they were Kleenex, and he left each one a little dirtier than he'd found her. Quinn tried to imagine what her father would say if he opened the door to his house and saw Puck, with his look-at-me Mohawk and his sexy smirk. He'd throw Quinn into a chastity belt. 'Besides, I'm dating Finn now.'

Puck leaned against the opposite wall. His jeans hung on his lean hips, and his long-sleeved thermal shirt hugged his pectorals. Quinn tried not to think of him showering off after football practice. 'That's official?'

Quinn nodded. 'Pretty much.' She took a deep breath,

feeling the need to lash out at Puck in some way. She needed to end this crazy, insane thing between them, and she'd already proved that she couldn't be trusted with him. 'We're probably even going to win homecoming king and queen. Everyone keeps telling me so, at least.'

Puck waved his hand in front of him and gave a brief, sarcastic bow. 'Well, I wouldn't want to stand between you and your crown, if that's what gets you all hot and bothered.'

'You're disgusting.' Quinn shifted her backpack on her shoulder. 'I don't know why I even came here.'

'Because you like me.' Puck stepped closer, so close she could see how long his eyelashes were. 'You can't say no to me.'

'How's this for no?' she asked, zipping up her white hooded sweater. It was warm in the closet, but she felt that she needed another layer of protection between her and Puck. 'Whatever this was between us, it's over. For real.'

Before he could say anything else, she opened the door. The hallway was completely empty, and she quickly walked away from the broom closet, hoping Puck would have enough sense to stay inside until she was gone, at least. Besides, she didn't really want to see him again. Not now. She paused, realizing exactly how late she was to English class, and then ducked into the girls' bathroom. She still needed a minute to collect herself.

Back in English class, Mr Horn perched on the corner of his desk and started telling the class about his trip to the south of France four years ago. They had just read – or pretended to read – the F. Scott Fitzgerald novel *Tender Is the Night*, which takes place on the French Riviera, so it was ostensibly relevant. The class was used to this sort of 'educational digression' from their teacher, and they all leaned back in their chairs and managed to carry on their own conversations without his ever noticing.

Santana glanced at the giant clock above the blackboard. What had happened to Quinn? She kept disappearing! The other day she'd been ten minutes late for Celibacy Club, which Santana had joined only at Quinn's insistence. And now she was way late for class. It was unlike her. Besides, Santana had brought her copy of *Lucky* magazine, covered in little sticky notes to mark the pages, and wanted advice on a dress for the homecoming dance. Mr Horn was babbling on about the farmers' markets in France, and it was the perfect opportunity for Quinn to help her decide on red, to make her pop, or dark green, to highlight her olive skin tone.

Bored, Santana scanned the room. Puck wasn't in class, either, which was much less surprising. He didn't always make it to class, and when he didn't, Santana found herself un-tethered. Who was she supposed to stare at now? He always sat one row over and two seats up, and Santana had the perfect angle to contemplate how sexy she found the back of his ears.

The door to the classroom opened a crack. Santana watched as Quinn crept into the room and slid into the seat behind

Santana. Mr Horn remained oblivious. He'd brought slides and was fiddling with the borrowed projector from the AV room.

'What took you so long?' Santana whispered over her shoulder. Her eyes scanned Quinn's face, which seemed unnaturally flushed.

Quinn didn't answer. Instead, she stretched forward and pointed at Santana's magazine. 'Ooh, is that the new issue? I saw this one dress that would look awesome on you. Let me find it.'

Santana handed over the magazine, already forgetting about the strange look in Quinn's eyes. And her smudged lip gloss.

thirteen

Choir room, Thursday after school

On Thursday after school, the windows to the choir room were open, and the sounds of whistle-blowing at practices and the faint hum of a lawn mower spilled into the room. Kurt was perched on the piano bench, his fingers absentmindedly playing the tune of 'How Do You Solve a Problem Like Maria?' from one of his favorite musicals, *The Sound of Music*, on the shiny black grand piano. He used to dream of being one of the Von Trapp kids – it seemed like a perfect existence to live in a house where songs were sung every night at bedtime. (In fact, one of the beautiful blond children in the movie had been named Kurt – although it was the older brother, Friedrich, on whom Kurt had always had a crush.) Perfect, that is, until the Nazis came and ruined everything.

Artie glanced at the clock on the wall. Mercedes and Rachel were running late, and the jazz band practiced in the choir room after Glee. A couple of guitars were already set up. 'Man, where are they?' His palms started to sweat every time he thought about the upcoming show. It was their last day of practice before D-day, and of course Artie was nervous. Terrified, actually. Did he really want to go onstage in front of the entire school? Everyone already hated him. Even the people who didn't think he was a total nerd treated him as if he were some kind of leper, as if being in a wheelchair was somehow contagious. But that's what made him want to do this, too. He wanted to get up there onstage and show them all that there was something he was good at. Maybe he was permanently excused from gym class because he could never kick a ball or jump a rope, but he could sing.

'Did you hear Rachel on the announcements this morning?' Tina asked. She was wearing a metal-studded headband and a T-shirt with Hello Kitty on it. Her eyelids were colored a glittery electric blue. She was drawing something on the inside of her arm with a green Sharpie. 'Either I'm becoming desensitized to her, or she's getting less annoying.' She lifted the tip of the marker.

'Desensitized.' Kurt paused his piano playing briefly. 'Definitely.'

'Hey, that's really good.' Artie wheeled closer to Tina's chair. The drawing that covered her arm was a picture of a phoenix, its wings spread triumphantly. He looked around for a magazine picture or something that she could have copied it from. 'Did you just, you know, invent that? Like, draw it out of the air?'

'Yeah.' Tina blushed. She'd always been good at copying pictures she'd seen, even once they were no longer in front of her. When she was a kid, she would fill sketchbooks with doodles of things she'd seen that day – animals, people, litter, whatever. Even now her notebooks were filled with sketches. It gave her something to do when she was trying not to be noticed.

'You're an amazing artist. I had no idea.'

'Th-th-thank you,' Tina mumbled. Artie was so nice. She wondered if maybe he'd had the time to change his mind about going to the dance. She twirled a piece of hair around her forefinger. Maybe she should just ask him. Even if he didn't think of her like that, he wouldn't say no. He was too sweet for that. And then, who knew? Maybe they'd have fun.

'That is not going to work, princess.' The three of them stopped what they were doing and looked up. Mercedes, with a sour look on her face, stomped through the doorway, followed quickly by Rachel. It was clear they'd been arguing.

'Why not? It would be perfect.' Rachel tossed her pink JanSport backpack onto a chair. Kurt got up from the piano and walked over to Mercedes, automatically standing beside her. Rachel planted her hands on her hips in an I'm-not-backing-down pose. 'Mercedes and I were discussing costumes for tomorrow's performance, and I think we should go with a fifties theme.'

'Like, poodle skirts?' Tina asked, skeptical.

'Exactly!' Rachel smiled. 'One of my dads is an active participant in Lima's community theater and, as you probably remember, the summer production was *Grease*. I'm sure we could borrow their poodle skirts.'

'And for the gentlemen?' Kurt asked. Even he wouldn't be caught dead in a poodle skirt.

'Something simple and James Dean–ish. Slim black jeans, white T-shirts.' She glanced at Artie and Kurt. 'Greased hair. You don't happen to have leather jackets, do you?'

'Look, we're not getting up onstage looking like rejects from your gramma's performance of *Grease*. That's just lame.' Mercedes waved her arms. 'Poodle skirts and saddle shoes. That's so middle school.'

'And what do you suggest?' Rachel asked, tucking her hair behind her ear. Out of everyone in Glee Club, she was the only one with any training in performing arts. She'd been in a series of pageants as a child – always excelling at the talent portion – and she only stopped when one of her dads spotted one of the other seven-year-olds forcing herself to vomit in the greenroom. But Rachel knew that appearances were very important, and it was essential to present a unified front. And who didn't smile at the sight of a poodle skirt?

'Something classier, maybe a little flashy.' Mercedes closed her eyes. When she thought of a great performer, she always pictured Madonna. Not that she thought they should all go out there dressed in catsuits and pointy bras, but they needed to do something dramatic.

'The theater department has some rhinestoned vests from last spring's musical.' Kurt's face lit up at the thought.

'Maybe with black T-shirts?' Tina suggested. 'And slim black pants, like Rachel said.'

Rachel sniffed. She knew Tina was just trying to placate her. Of course they were going against her fifties-theme idea. She had suggested it, after all, and they resented her. Maybe because she was late to join their group or because they were jealous of her talent. Either way, they were all determined to stand in the way of her career. 'Fine.'

Mercedes glanced at Rachel. She was glad she'd won their argument, but she didn't want to completely piss off Rachel and make her quit. 'I don't think I could rock a poodle skirt with this bod, anyway.'

Rachel forced a smile. 'Let's just practice,' she said primly. 'We still haven't nailed all those moves. Kurt, you keep leading with the wrong foot.'

Kurt gave her a brief salute. 'Yes, Captain.'

Rachel sighed and then cued them to take it from the top. There was no point in getting upset about this. She probably wasn't going to be at McKinley much longer. And while it would be satisfying to tell them all that, she wanted to make sure they would still listen to her directions for the performance.

She needed this performance to rock the house – she wanted to go out with a bang.

fourteen

McKinley High hallway, Thursday after school

'**D**o you think Rachel really knows every single word in *West Side Story*?' Tina asked Artie as the two of them, both exhausted, left Glee Club practice. While Rachel was whipping them into fighting shape, as she called it, she claimed that in the second grade she'd memorized the complete lyrics to her favorite musical.

'It wouldn't surprise me,' Artie said. 'She strikes me as the obsessive type.'

Tina giggled. She untied her black hoodie from around her waist and slid her arms into the sleeves. 'It's a really long musical.'

'It still wouldn't surprise me.' Artie smiled and stopped. 'I've got to go this way.' He tilted his head toward the back entrance of the school, the one that let out behind the cafeteria. 'My dad's picking me up.'

'Why does he pick you up out there?' Tina asked, wrinkling her nose. 'Isn't that where all the grease Dumpsters are?' It always smelled like burned fish sticks in the hallway behind the cafeteria, even when they weren't on that day's menu. Her mother was picking her up at the circular driveway near the front entrance of the school. Tina usually took the bus home after school, but when she stayed later for Glee, she managed to escape that humiliation.

Artie laughed ruefully. 'It's also the only exit with a handi-cap ramp.' He shrugged. 'It's how I always come and go.'

Tina flushed bright red. 'I'm s-s-sorry,' she stuttered. She wondered if Artie thought she was a total idiot. She was always saying stupid things around him because she was so used to his being in a wheelchair that she didn't even think about it anymore. 'I didn't realize.'

'No worries.' Artie waved his hand to show it was no big deal. He was so accustomed to going out the back entrance of the school that the smell of fish sticks didn't even bother him. He'd actually never used the front entrance, as it was accessible only by a set of five wide concrete steps that someone would have had to carry him up. But he was used to seeing things from different angles than everyone else. 'Rest your vocal cords tonight. We've got a show tomorrow.'

Tina watched Artie wheel away. When she turned around, she was facing a bright yellow sign hanging on the wall:

Tina stared at the poster, which was surprisingly lame. The only decoration on it was a clip-art paintbrush glued onto the poster board. If the decorations committee was really that unskilled, it definitely could use as many artists as it could get. Maybe because Artie had just called her an amazing artist during Glee Club, she was starting to think she had something artistic to offer.

Besides, even though Rachel was annoying, what she had said the other day was stuck in Tina's head. Why shouldn't people like her be allowed to get involved in extracurricular activities? The popular kids shouldn't have a monopoly on everything. She had just as much right as anyone else to work on the decorations.

'Move it, Goth girl.' A couple of guys on the swim team brushed past her, their gym bags bumping into her. They reeked of chlorine, and the smell stung Tina's eyes.

Usually, she shied away from doing anything that required interaction with other students. That was why, way back in sixth grade, she'd first faked a stutter. It was her turn to give a presentation on something – the Missouri Compromise – and she hadn't been able to sleep the night before. It was the first time someone had asked her to stand in front of the class and talk – for five minutes, which seemed like an eternity – and it terrified her. When she got to the front of the

117

classroom, she pulled aside Mrs Marcy and told her, tearfully, that she couldn't do the presentation because...she was t-t-too ashamed of her s-s-stutter. If Mrs Marcy hadn't noticed the stutter until that point, it wasn't really her fault – Tina was already inclined toward silence, and the class had more than thirty-five kids in it.

But the results were phenomenal. Tina had just wanted to get out of one stupid presentation; instead, she was given a virtual free pass for *all* future presentations. When she had to work on group projects, she'd always be the one to do the research while the others presented the results. She started to rely on the stutter as a shield – no one expected her to be socially active with a speech impediment, so she was allowed to become the loner she'd always been, preferring to doodle and sketch instead of talk to other kids. And she'd been fine with that, most of the time. It was easier and safer that way.

Recently, though, she felt like a hermit crab that was slowly realizing it was time to come out of its shell and stretch its arms out to see what it could do. (Did hermit crabs have arms? Or were they just claws?)

Maybe it was that Glee Club was finally starting to show a glimmer of promise, or maybe it was something in those new multivitamins her mom had started her on, but Tina was feeling...unstoppable. Without any second thoughts, she grabbed the Sharpie from her backpack, popped off the cap, and signed her name on the list. She was artistic, and she knew she could help.

And maybe, in the back of her mind, she was hoping that this would be the thing that would make Artie want to go to the homecoming dance. Would he be so curious about her decorations that he'd be willing to attend a potentially lame school function? A girl could hope.

fifteen

Rachel's house, Thursday night

Rachel Berry loaded the family's lime-green dishes into the dishwasher. She and her two dads alternated dinner chores, which mostly consisted of ordering out and cleaning up. Tonight had been Rachel's turn to cook. She'd made – from a recipe in their well-used Martha Stewart cookbook – a scrumptious tuna tartare over mesclun greens, with a side of grilled asparagus and roasted red potatoes. Cooking was just mundane enough to take the edge off – and Rachel knew she needed to relax tonight to get ready for the big performance tomorrow.

Usually, whoever had cooked escaped doing the dishes, but Thursday night happened to coincide with the nineteen-year anniversary of the day her dads first met, and they had plans to head to the old revival theater downtown for a one-night-only screening of *Some Like It Hot.*

'You sure you don't want to come?' her dad Leroy asked, peeping his head into the kitchen as Rachel washed the table with a soapy sponge. He was African-American, which Rachel felt entitled her to join the Minority Students Coalition at school. She loved beefing up her résumé with extracurriculars.

'You guys go out and have a fun date night.' Rachel plucked a white petal that had fallen from the vase of two dozen roses she'd given her dads that morning. 'I have a lot of homework, and I need to do my relaxation exercises to prepare for the recital tomorrow.'

'You're going to be so great.' Rachel's other dad, Hiram, breezed into the kitchen and grabbed his black leather wallet from the counter. He gave her a quick peck on the cheek. 'Don't work too hard.'

Soon Rachel heard the sound of the Subaru pulling out of the garage. It was nice to have the house to herself, although it made her wish she had a boyfriend whom she could text to come over for an impromptu make-out session. She'd only kissed a couple of boys, at performing arts camp, and one of them had decided he was gay after kissing Rachel. She knew she was an attractive, talented young woman with an excellent sense of humor and perfectly straight white teeth – in other words, a real catch. Unfortunately, the only boys at McKinley who might have agreed with her were the ones she couldn't ever imagine kissing.

Rachel sighed and plunked herself down at her white wood desk. Later she would take a lavender-scented bubble bath and do her visualizations. She'd taken a workshop at the community college with a motivation therapist, and now Rachel was devoted to visualizing future events exactly as she wanted them to play out. The auditorium tomorrow, dimly lit. The audience members, holding their breath. Then a light shines on Rachel – and, she guesses, the other Glee kids, although they're more in the background. She opens her mouth, and her voice fills the room. Thunderous applause.

Maybe visualization was silly, but it couldn't hurt. But before she could visualize, she had to update her MySpace page. She was addicted. It was an excellent tool for marketing her musical talents. All sorts of singers and bands had got record deals because they started building a fan base from the ground up, and Rachel was devoted to posting a new video or sound clip every day.

She clicked her remote, and her iPod docking station turned on. She selected her Powerful Ladies playlist, and Gwen Stefani's voice flooded the room. Rachel's room, with its sunshine-yellow walls, tailored bedspread, and giant beanbag chair in the corner, never failed to cheer her up. This was where she did her best work – she'd just filmed herself singing Leona Lewis's 'Bleeding Love' that afternoon, and the video was good.

After deleting a few spam comments from some Cheerios who had too much time on their hands, and from some creepy guy telling her she had beautiful tonsils, Rachel proceeded to upload her video. Every time she clicked UPLOAD she felt a thrill of excitement – discovery could be only a click away. All it would take was one well-connected person who knew something about talent to see Rachel and be blown away, and then her life could unfold before her like a magical red carpet.

Rachel was about to concentrate on her history homework, when a bleep notified her that she had an instant message. A window popped up with a message from Sharkfinn5: *P.S. Be careful at the show tomorrow. Some Cheerios are planning some sort of prank. From a stranger.*

Rachel stared at the screen. Within three seconds, she realized the IM had to be from Finn Hudson. The spelling of the screen name – two *n*'s – combined with his football number and the incorrectly used *P.S.* (you couldn't have a postscript if nothing preceded it) all pointed to him. Besides, who else could know what the Cheerios were up to except an insider like him? And she knew they'd had a 'moment' in the auditorium the other day. She hadn't imagined that. Her fingers started to tingle. Finn Hudson was concerned about what happened to *her*!

He was going against his ranks and facing potential censure to warn her? He was betraying the Cheerios' – and his girlfriend Quinn's – confidence just because he was worried about Rachel?

Thanks for the warning, stranger, she typed. *But what kind of prank can I expect?*

A minute passed by, then two. Rachel didn't think he was going to respond. Then suddenly an IM popped up: *I don't know. I just had to say something. Bye.*

Rachel stared at the screen. She didn't want to write anything more and freak Finn out. He clearly thought he was being sneaky and warning her anonymously. He might not be the sharpest crayon in the box, but he was sweet, at least. And very cute.

This was an interesting turn of events. She should have known that her assault on the Cheerios' homecoming voting scam wouldn't go unpunished. Now that she thought of it, it did seem strange that she hadn't been slushied yet for her dissent. The Cheerios must be up to something.

But the joy Rachel felt at knowing that Finn had reached out to her made it hard to take the threat seriously. She decided to change into her pajamas to think it all over. She often thought more clearly when wearing her most comfortable clothing. She pulled a pair of neatly folded pink-and-white-striped jammies from her top drawer and quickly stepped into them, tossing her other clothes into the white wicker laundry hamper.

As she saw it, she had two choices: first, she could warn the other Glee kids of the intel she'd received about the possible attack during the show. If they knew, they would probably back out of the performance instead of take their chances. She had to face it – they were wimps. They didn't have any of Rachel's can-do attitude.

Which brought her to her second option. She needed the performing experience to improve herself, and here was the opportunity to go onstage tomorrow and show the world her stuff. And she liked – okay, she *loved* – being the center of attention. In fact, she thrived on it. Being onstage the other day, with Finn watching her from the dark auditorium, had felt so good. She closed her eyes and could feel the wooden floorboards of the stage beneath her feet. She could hear the rustling of the crowd as they waited for the Glee kids to come onstage, and their silence when the singers finally stepped out.

She could see the awestruck looks on their faces as they stared at her and wondered what McKinley High had been hiding all this time.

Her choice was pretty clear. The show must go on.

sixteen

McKinley High gym, Friday during school

Friday morning, Tina grabbed her skull-and-bones messenger bag and rushed out of biology lab the second the bell rang. Three days a week she had biology lab right before lunch, which seemed like a recipe for disaster when they were doing dissections. Mercedes, who sat in front of her, had moved even faster.

'Whose brilliant idea was it to require all students to know how to dissect a frog before they can graduate?' Mercedes complained, fanning her face with a purple notebook. 'Has Mr Rochna never heard of online learning? I totally found a frog dissection tutorial last night.'

Tina glanced at her friend, whose face looked a sickly green. Mercedes was Tina's lab partner, and even though Tina had offered to make all the incisions, Mr Rochna had come over and insisted that Mercedes be the one to remove the kidneys. She'd almost hurled all over the dissection table. 'That doesn't sound much better.'

'Are you serious? I can deal with froggie insides when they're not stretched out in front of me. How am I supposed to eat lunch now?' Mercedes continued. 'All I can smell is frog guts.'

Tina giggled. She didn't totally mind the dissections, and Mercedes entertained her when she overreacted. It was kind of interesting, in a gross way, to see the secret inner workings of something. The frogs themselves were pretty icky – much longer than any frog Tina had ever seen swimming around in her aboveground pool or jumping into her neighbors' koi pond. 'I'm actually not going to lunch today,' Tina spoke up. 'I'm going to a decorations committee meeting in the gym.'

Mercedes stopped in her tracks. Her eyes bugged out. Tina was interested in doing something social? 'Clearly, I didn't hear you right. Repeat.'

Tina repeated what she had said, this time with a stutter.

'For the homecoming dance?' Mercedes asked slowly. She finally started to walk again when some soccer guys walked by tossing a stolen dead frog back and forth. 'Oh my God, I've got to get out of this school.'

'Yeah.' Tina shrugged, glad Mercedes was distracted. She always had strong opinions on things, and if Mercedes told

Tina that joining the decorations committee was a big mistake, Tina might have listened. 'I thought it would be fun.'

Mercedes nodded slowly. Her huge brown eyes glanced at Tina. 'Don't let them push you around.' She waved a finger back and forth in the air. 'Lena Horne didn't let people push her around.'

When Tina got to the gym, she paused in the open doorway. It was as unexciting as any school gym. It had rows of bleachers that folded back against one long wall, enormously tall ceilings lined with frosted-glass windows, and all sorts of structural beams and apparatuses on the ceiling that seemed to do nothing but raise and lower the basketball nets. The gymnasium smelled like sweat and the rubber of basketballs, and it always reminded Tina of elementary school, when they used to play dodgeball (Who had decided *that* was a good idea?) and she was always being hit with the red rubber ball that, even though it was supposed to be soft, really hurt when someone whipped it at your face.

She took a deep breath and fought the urge to flee.

Sitting in the corner of the bleachers was the decorations committee, which appeared to consist mostly of Cheerios and girls who wanted to be Cheerios someday. There were no boys, just a dozen or so girls in various states of repose, checking their phones and playing with their iPods. Several giant cardboard boxes sat on the gym floor; they looked as though they'd been pulled out of the basement, where they'd lived for the last two hundred years. One girl was braiding another's hair while someone else braided hers.

This was the decorations committee? For some reason, the appearance of incredible incompetence inspired Tina. She could definitely bring something to this group.

The girls looked up as Tina's Doc Martens squeaked across the shiny gym floorboards. Why did they have to polish the floor so much? It looked like you could skate on it. Tina concentrated on not stumbling, and she finally made it to the bleachers after what felt like eternity. She sat down on the lowest bleacher. 'H-h-hi,' she said, because everyone was looking at her expectantly. 'I'm here for the meeting.'

'Right.' Santana Lopez exchanged glances with Kirsten Niedenhoffer, a curvy blond senior who was on strict instructions from Coach Sylvester to lose ten pounds or she could no longer be in the second tier of the Cheerios' pyramid.

'We were just about to get started,' Kirsten declared authoritatively. She'd volunteered to lead the meeting. 'As we all know, the homecoming dance is an extremely essential social function at McKinley, and it is absolutely crucial that the decorations are suitably cool.'

Santana stared at the girl who'd just sat down. She was wearing black jeans with giant holes in the knees, a white tank top, and a blue-and-black plaid flannel shirt that matched the blue streaks in her hair. Her boots looked like combat boots. Had no one told her that Goth was so over? What was she even doing here? Santana knew it had been a mistake to advertise the meeting. Anyone who was anyone already knew about it.

Tina let her eyes wander around the gymnasium as Kirsten continued with her opening remarks. Tina found it hard to imagine the space as anything other than a place where she was constantly humiliated each time Ms Tuft, the girls' gym teacher, insisted that Tina try to serve the volleyball and it *thwock*ed someone's head instead of soaring over the net. But she tried to imagine the lights turned down low, with maybe just a little moonlight coming through the high windows and shining onto the dance floor as couples swayed back and forth. She pictured golds and silvers, the colors of sunlight and moonlight, hanging and draping down from above.

'We need some volunteers to be responsible for decorating the stage, where the king and queen will be crowned,' Kirsten continued. 'I don't need to tell you how important this is.'

A few Cheerios raised their hands to volunteer, as did Tina. Not that she cared about the king and queen's coronation stage – she just wanted to show that she was up for anything. 'Okay, Alice, Olivia, and Olivia K, you three can be in charge of that.' Kirsten consulted the list she was holding in her hand. 'Next, we need some people to come up with ideas for what to stretch back and forth across the gym. Lights? Streamers? Who wants to do that?'

Tina raised her hand again, but again Kirsten didn't seem to notice her. 'We'll need some volunteers to take charge of the walls – how can we cover up those awful mats?' She pointed at a few people and instructed them to head over to the walls and try to figure out what to do. Tina glanced around her. No one seemed to be too concerned about their tasks, and Kirsten had even paused in her directions to respond to a text message.

Tina stood up and then crouched next to the closest box on the gym floor. It was covered in mildew and smelled like Tina's grandma's basement. The box contained dozens and dozens of cardboard palm trees and cutouts of hula girls for what must have been a Hawaiian-themed occasion. Lame.

She had more luck with the next box. She opened it up to find hundreds of cool-looking cutout stars of varying sizes, although they had seen better days. Some were giant, almost as big as the box itself, and others were smaller and more delicate. They'd been made with a thick kind of cardboard that had warped slightly with time, and the gold paint was faded and chipped in spots. Still, maybe Tina could do some-thing with them. Maybe she could flatten them out and cover them with glittery spray paint.

Suddenly she felt excited. She could contribute to this, after all.

She took a star over to Kirsten, who was chewing on a carrot stick and talking to Santana. 'Do you think I could work on f-f-fixing these stars?' Tina asked. 'There are hundreds of them, and we c-c-could, like, hang gold stars everywhere.'

Kirsten smiled sweetly. 'Sure,' she said in the voice she

used with her annoying twelve-year-old brother. 'You go ahead and do that.'

Tina nodded her head. She knew that Kirsten was just patronizing her, but she didn't care. She could already picture the gym, glittery and un-gymlike, and she imagined Artie telling her, again, what an amazing artist she was. What an amazing *girl* she was.

Tina eagerly went back to dig through the boxes, checking for any other gems. She started to sing under her breath as she lifted star after star, looking for the least-damaged ones.

'Right, loser.' Kirsten shook her head as she watched Tina walk away in her clunky black boots. 'Like we're going to do anything you say.'

Santana just stared at Tina. How did she know that girl? It's not like she paid attention to people like that. Then it hit her – when she'd walked past the music room the other day, she'd heard some people singing a lame old Broadway show song that her dad always sang to her mother. Santana had poked her head in the room and had almost thrown up. Annoying Rachel Berry was bossing everyone around, telling them to sing certain parts over again, and Tina had been one of the girls. 'She's in Glee,' Santana whispered to Kirsten.

Kirsten's blue eyes widened. 'Oooooooh.' She lowered her voice. 'What are you going to do?'

'Watch.' Santana got to her feet. Next to the boxes of decorations that the janitor had cleared out of storage for them – he told them to use what they wanted, and he'd incinerate the rest – was a box holding an old fog machine. The Cheerios had tried to use it in practice the day before, during their Black Eyed Peas 'Don't Phunk with My Heart' number, but it was crappy and practically toxic, belching out large, thick clouds of smoke. They'd all started coughing and had to take five, to Coach Sylvester's chagrin, until the smoke had cleared the field. And that was outside. Santana could imagine what the machine would do indoors, in an enclosed auditorium, onstage, while a certain annoying someone and her friends were trying to perform for the whole school. She and Quinn had already decided to somehow turn it on while the Glee Club was performing, but it would be even better if she could give it to Tina now and have her turn it on herself.

Santana picked up the box and walked over to Tina. She made her face look innocent and helpful. 'Hey,' she said, because she didn't know Tina's name. 'You're performing tonight, right?'

Tina dropped the stars she was holding. They cascaded over the gym floor. Tina bent down to pick them up and, much to her surprise, so did Santana. The Cheerio grabbed a couple of stars with her free hand. With the other, she clutched a box to her side. 'Yes. W-w-with Glee Club,' Tina replied.

'I just thought you might want to use this fog machine during the performance.' Santana tried to smile sweetly. She could act – she'd had three lines in McKinley High's spring performance of *Anything Goes*, and her mother said she was very convincing as 'Old Lady with Monocle'. 'We used it at practice the other day, and it had a really awesome effect. It would look super-professional if you had someone run it during your performance.'

Tina stared at the box Santana was holding. This was weird.

But also nice. Maybe the Cheerios weren't as bad as she'd thought. Even if they hadn't exactly paid attention to her at the meeting, they hadn't slushied her or called her names or anything. Santana had even bent down to pick up some of the stars Tina dropped – that was a nice, normal gesture that Tina never would have expected from a Cheerio. And now Santana was actually sharing Cheerios' equipment with her?

'Th-th-that's really nice of you.' Tina dropped the stars back into the box and took the fog machine from Santana's hands. She could already picture the fog billowing out onstage, and then the Glee Club emerging from it, singing in their rhinestoned uniforms. It was going to be awesome. 'Thanks.'

'No problem whatsoever,' Santana replied, spinning on the toe of her sneaker. This was going to be even better than she'd imagined.

Maybe once Rachel Berry realized who she was messing with, she'd learn to keep her mouth shut.

seventeen

McKinley High auditorium, Friday night

Nervous tension hung in the air like heavy fog on Friday night as the Glee kids huddled together backstage before the start of the Fall in Love with Music recital. There wasn't a real greenroom, and so students with instruments crowded in the wings, trying not to get their guitars tangled in the long cords that pulled the weighty maroon curtains back and forth across the stage. Jazz band members stuck reeds in their mouths and polished their instruments. A boy named Jacob, whose frizzy mop of light brown hair had earned him the dubious nickname 'J-Fro', was acting as one of the stagehands. He carried a clipboard and was going from group to group, making sure everyone was present. He wore a thick black tie over his short-sleeved blue button-down, the armpits already damp, for the occasion.

Rachel stood near a background wall painted with a scene of a Russian dacha in the countryside from an old performance of *Fiddler on the Roof*. She'd scouted the entire backstage area for Cheerios, but she hadn't spotted a single one lurking among the music kids and plotting against Glee. Maybe Finn had been wrong. That was entirely possible, as he didn't seem to always have his thumb on what was going on.

Or, more likely, the Cheerios were just all talk. What could they do, anyway? Nasty, blatantly false rumors about Rachel were already Sharpied across bathroom stalls. Maybe the cheerleaders had just planted the rumor of a planned prank to mess with Rachel's head. That was it. Well, that wasn't going to happen.

She closed her eyes and blew air out her mouth, letting her lips vibrate and make a *brbrbr* sound.

'Is she blowing kisses to her imaginary lover?' Kurt whispered not too softly in Mercedes's ear. In his black American Apparel shirt and his slim-fitting Armani pants, he knew he looked good.

'It's called a lip trill, or "the bubble", as my old voice instructor liked to call it.' Rachel quickly turned to Kurt. 'It's an extremely useful warm-up exercise for any singer, whether to warm up before a performance' – Rachel made a grand gesture with her arm to indicate that that's what she was doing now, in case they couldn't tell – 'or to build a strong and healthy voice.' Her eyes landed on Kurt, Mercedes, and

Artie in turn. 'You might all want to try incorporating it into your vocal warm-ups.'

'Where is Tina?' Mercedes pointedly turned her back to Rachel. It would do no good to lose her temper now. Besides, they had a more pressing issue if Tina wasn't here. For a moment, her eyes got wide as she thought of how terrified Tina had been last year in Spanish class when Mr Schuester had made them all act out a skit of 'The Three Little Pigs', or '*Los tres cerditos*'. Mercedes had been thrilled to play *Cerdito número dos*. Tina, however, had been terrified of her role as a tree with no lines, and she'd skipped class the day they were supposed to put on the skit for a group of elementary school kids. 'It had better not be "*Los tres cerditos*" again.'

'It's all falling apart, isn't it?' Kurt asked, his eyes glazing over. 'I'd prefer it if we fled now, rather than be humiliated onstage.'

'She'll be here.' Someone almost tripped over Artie's wheelchair. He rolled backward, bumping into a table with a plastic vase with fake flowers glued inside.

'Nice outfits.' Jacob appeared suddenly at Rachel's right, close enough that she could smell his deodorant – which, judging by the growing sweat stains under his arms, was not strong enough. She took a step back. 'You look very dazzling,' he added.

'Thank you.' Rachel smiled at Kurt diplomatically. While his wardrobe scouting was industrious, the effect of the whole group wearing identical vests had come off as – she hated to admit it – slightly nerdy. She'd worn her pleated black miniskirt, which she knew highlighted her legs, shapely from the hours she spent each week on her elliptical trainer. Even though her outfit selection was limited to things black, it had taken her an hour to get dressed. This would be her first performance – of many, she hoped – in front of her McKinley High peers, and she wanted it to go perfectly. She'd chosen her favorite black T-shirt with the puff sleeves, and she'd worn her favorite bra-and-panties set – white cotton, covered in gold stars – for an extra boost of confidence. Not that she really needed it. They were going to be great.

'I don't know.' Artie glanced down at his vest, which he'd put on over a black T-shirt, as instructed, and his black suspenders. The rhinestones were awfully glittery. Maybe it hadn't been the greatest idea to let Kurt, who'd once come to school in a rabbit fur coat, take charge of their costumes. 'I feel like my aunt Linda has this exact same vest.'

'Your aunt Linda must be a style icon, then.' Kurt threw his shoulders back. To carry off the BeDazzled look well, confidence was a must. 'We look awesome.'

'Rachel, I do think the vest accentuates some of your best assets.' Jacob grinned nervously at Rachel as he pushed his thick black glasses into place on the bridge of his nose.

Ew, she thought. Just because they had the Jewish religion in common did not mean Rachel Berry owed skeezy Jacob anything. The fact, however, that he wrote a blog reporting on all matters of McKinley High life made Rachel behave a little more kindly to him than if he'd been completely useless to her. It never paid to be rude to the press. And the Glee Club could use a good review. 'What are you doing here, Jacob?' Rachel asked, crossing her arms over her chest and trying to keep the annoyance in her voice to a minimum.

Jacob looked back to his clipboard. 'Making sure every group is ready. Are you all here?'

'Yes, we're all here!' Tina's cried out as she appeared, pushing past a tuba player in a top hat. 'I'm sorry I'm so late.' She was lugging the box with the fog machine in it and practically panting. 'But I brought a present.'

'What is that?' Rachel asked, curiously peering into the box. She hated surprises.

'It's a f-f-fog machine,' Tina announced proudly. 'It was with all the boxes of decorations at the decorations committee meeting.'

Rachel gasped. 'That is so crazy. I had this dream last night where I was performing at this exact recital, singing 'On My Own' from *Les Misérables*, and the fog started to rise up around me, like I was on the streets of Paris while it was under siege.' Rachel had a faraway look in her eyes. Why hadn't she thought to mention a fog machine for their performance? She would have loved to take the credit for it.

'Notice the lack of any of us in her dream/fantasy,' Kurt whispered to Mercedes. 'Not that I'd feel comfortable if she was having nocturnal fantasies about me.'

'It sounds really awesome, but how are we going to run it?' Artie asked.

'I can help,' Jacob volunteered, seeing how excited Rachel was at the thought of the fog machine. Maybe that's what it would take to get in her pants. 'I was the prop manager for three of the last four school productions. I know where all the electrical outlets are.'

Tina handed him the box and dusted off her rhinestone vest. She was wearing a black skirt, black kneesocks, and her beloved Doc Marten Mary Janes. 'I'll show you how to use it.' Jacob and the others watched as Tina set up the machine. It whirred to life when plugged in. 'Just point it at the stage, and push this r-r-red button down for ten seconds at a time.' She glanced at Jacob, suddenly dubious. 'Can you do that?' Kids rushed around, shoving each other and shouting about amps and receivers. The Glee kids stepped out of the way, trying to let the sounds of Rachel humming and doing other weird vocal exercises soothe them.

Jacob glanced at Rachel, who was doing the sexy *brbrbr* thing with her lips again. He moistened his own lips and rubbed them together. 'Most definitely.'

But when the jazz band, the opening act, burst into Glenn Miller's 'In the Mood', the reality of the situation started to sink in. Artie leaned back in his chair and breathed into his cupped palms, trying not to hyperventilate.

'Are you okay, Artie?' Tina asked, leaning over him. His cheeks looked blue.

'I...I think maybe we're rushing into this performance thing.' He glanced down at his rhinestone vest, wishing he had the comfort of his regular white button-down shirt and suspenders. This felt all wrong. 'I mean, how much have we really practiced? Do you think we can really go out there and not embarrass ourselves?'

Tina felt the familiar panic rise in her. It was like when her older sister used to sit on her chest and tickle her stomach until she started to turn blue. How could she sing – in front of everyone – when she felt like she was going to choke? 'Maybe Artie's right.'

'Look, why don't we just turn around right now before we make a big mistake?' Mercedes pictured the comfort of her own living room, with the huge leather sectional and the flat-screen TV. 'We could all go to my house and laugh at *High School Musical*.'

'Don't slam Zac Efron,' Kurt warned. 'That boy has perfect hair.'

Rachel's mouth had fallen almost to the floor. 'Those kids suck,' she declared. 'I can't even believe you'd consider backing out right now. That sort of attitude is what has prevented you from being a great Glee Club thus far.' She took a deep breath. Just being backstage, waiting in the wings for her chance in the spotlight, made all Rachel's nerves tingle. The hot lights out on the stage, the polite clapping of the audience as the jazz band completed its first number, the way the red EXIT signs above the back doors of the auditorium stood out in the darkness – they all just made her want it more.

'But we're scared—' Mercedes started.

Rachel cut her off. 'Everyone gets scared. You all need to suck it up. As the incomparable Cher once said, "Until you're ready to look foolish, you'll never have the possibility of being great."'

Rachel's words did the trick. Immediately, Artie stopped hyperventilating, and Tina felt as if she'd shoved her sister off her chest. Kurt and Mercedes were nodding. Rachel was right.

'You're next,' Jacob hissed to them after the performance of a two-person band called Righteous Annihilation. 'Get out there!'

Rachel didn't hesitate, and the others followed her across the stage in the darkness. The audience was relatively sparse, filled mostly with parents of band kids, a few teachers, and a couple dozen students. Rachel immediately spotted her two dads, off to the left. Her dad Hiram was holding their mini-camcorder to his face.

But she didn't see the one person she was looking for – Finn. He had to show up, didn't he? He'd cared enough to warn her of a possible attack; wouldn't he come to make sure she was okay? And maybe, just maybe, when he saw her there onstage singing, it would take him back to that day in the auditorium, when they'd had their moment.

The music started. The spotlight clicked on, and they began to sing 'Tonight'. The fog billowed mystically around them, and Rachel couldn't help feeling proud of Tina for bringing the extra touch of showmanship to their performance. None of them had noticed a couple of Cheerios sneaking up the side aisle from the back of the auditorium and then disappearing backstage. They sounded...decent. Not great, but not bad, and certainly better than they had sounded before Rachel joined. By the end of the first verse, they started to get more into it, sounding even better.

But the fog was getting pretty thick. Tina had impressed upon J-Fro the necessity of turning the machine on and off in ten-second intervals to keep the air clear. But the stage was starting to fill up with smoke, as if he'd forgotten. Tina found herself almost tripping over Artie's footrest as she tried to follow the moves Rachel had taught them. But it was getting too hard to see much of anything.

Rachel sang out valiantly, managing to squint backstage. Jacob was standing next to the fog machine, all right, but he wasn't alone. Next to him, her blond hair cascading over her shoulders, was Brittany in her skimpy Cheerios outfit. In a move that looked like something from a beer commercial, she was applying lipstick to her lips in super-slow motion, and Jacob was completely mesmerized.

Rachel fought a cough. Tina had stopped singing and was trying to clear her throat. Rachel motioned with her hands toward the front of the stage, trying to get the others to step forward, where the air might be a little clearer.

That was a mistake. Kurt, unable to see the edge of the stage, fell right off it. An enormous crash ensued as he landed on a drum set in the orchestra pit. Tina screamed a high-pitched note as Artie rolled over her foot, and Mercedes, in an effort to help Kurt, fell face-first and slid along the stage.

'*What you are, what you do, what you say . . .*' Rachel, unfazed, was the only one who managed to sing the final line of the song. Her extensive vocal training must have prepared her for the challenges presented by the smoke inhalation. But she didn't feel good about it.

In the back of the auditorium, a bunch of Cheerios and football players were hunched over in laughter. The cheerleaders' high-pitched giggles were audible over the pitying applause of the audience. Then the jocks started to clap their hands loudly, mockingly.

The Glee kids, sans Kurt, rushed off the stage, humiliated.

Down on the auditorium floor, Kurt quickly made his way to the wings, almost stumbling over the music stands and chairs in the pit. But Rachel felt like she was moving in slow motion as she followed the others off the stage, waving her hands in front of her face to clear the air. She'd been laughed at before – that was nothing new. The other Glee kids, though, weren't as used to putting themselves out there as she was. They didn't have the iron backbone that Rachel had developed over the years. When confronted with a challenge, Rachel tended to take a deep breath and charge forward. She knew from spending the week with the Glee kids, however, that they were more likely to sit down and hope they could just disappear.

Rachel worried that Glee was doomed.

eighteen

Choir room, Monday morning

On Sunday night, after a long weekend of feeling sorry for herself, Rachel texted the other Glee kids and called an emergency meeting Monday morning in the choir room. She hadn't been able to bring herself to contact anyone else over the weekend, as she was too crushed by Glee's humiliation at the hands of the Cheerios. Instead, she watched a couple of her favorite movies, *A Star Is Born* and *Grease*, in her favorite flannel pajamas on the cushy couch in the living room and ate butter-flavored microwave popcorn until she started to feel better.

The performance had been terrible, and they hadn't even gotten to finish their song before they started coughing their lungs up. But Rachel watched the recording her dads had made before the fog overtook the stage and her dad Hiram had to leave the room because of his asthma, and she saw what the other acts had looked like. The jazz band was mediocre at best, and the three guys who had attempted to sing the latest Fray song while hitting some of the correct notes on their guitars were no better. The two members of Righteous Annihilation were jocks – both forwards on the McKinley soccer team – and the small audience clapped enthusiastically when they finished – the families because they were grateful the atrocious racket was over, and the students because they were willing to applaud anyone who knew where the good parties were each weekend.

When Rachel strolled into the choir room and saw the dejected faces of her fellow Gleeks, she knew she had a lot of work to do. 'Okay,' she said brightly, 'maybe the show didn't turn out exactly the way we wanted, but I think it was a good first step.'

'Were you even there on Friday?' Kurt asked, jumping to his feet. He'd taken off the pair of dark sunglasses he'd worn to school, hoping that perhaps the football guys wouldn't recognize him.

'I know the performance wasn't ideal,' Rachel continued, 'but I've watched a recording of the show, and we were really good.' She sniffed the air and thought she still smelled traces of smoke. 'For like ten seconds.'

'For ten seconds!' Mercedes exclaimed. Walking through the halls that morning, Mercedes had felt as if everyone was whispering about her. Even though there hadn't been many people in the audience – a fact that she was incredibly grateful for – she knew that the Cheerios had told everyone about their little prank to humiliate Glee. 'That's supposed to make us feel better?'

Artie and Tina exchanged glances. Kurt and Mercedes sounded like they wanted to jump down Rachel's throat. But Artie found himself kind of impressed with Rachel's resilience. She was wearing a yellow-and-brown plaid skirt, a white turtleneck sweater, kneesocks, and a brown beret. She looked like a Parisian Nancy Drew – peppy, determined, and ready to take on the world. He glanced at Tina, sitting next to him and nursing a Starbucks drink.

'But as Cher said...' Rachel pressed her hands together.

'I don't want to hear any more of your inspirational messages,' Mercedes interrupted. 'I don't know why we listened to you.' Mercedes shook her head. 'You might be okay with looking like a fool, but you shouldn't have taken us down with you.'

'Me?' Rachel squealed. She looked around the room and realized, for the first time, that everyone was angry with her. *Her*. After all she'd done to take this Glee Club to the top, this was the thanks she got. That was gratitude for you.

'If you hadn't pushed us with your blind ambition, we never would have embarrassed ourselves on that stage.' Kurt unscrewed the cap of his water bottle and took a sip. His pores were a mess today after a weekend of stressing out, and he could feel a giant underground pimple threatening to break out on his left cheek. 'We would have backed out days ago.'

'At least we knew our limits before you came along,' Artie finally spoke up. He felt like Kurt and Mercedes were partly right, at least. Just because Rachel knew she was an amazing performer didn't mean she knew anything about the rest of them.

'That's not fair.' Rachel felt as though she'd been slapped. Even Artie was mad at her? 'I pushed you hard because you needed it.' Rachel didn't believe a person could be pushed too hard – you could either rise to the occasion or let it defeat you.

Part of her knew she *was* to blame, at least in a teeny way, for the debacle, but she wasn't about to admit it, even to herself. Buried deep in her subconscious was the truth: Finn Hudson had warned her of what was going to happen, and she'd chosen to ignore it. If she'd just told the others about it, Tina might have realized that the 'gift' of the fog machine from the Cheerios wasn't made out of love but, rather, a jealous desire to ruin Rachel. But Rachel was not someone to plumb the depths of her subconscious, especially if doing so would reveal her own complicity.

Instead, she turned to Tina. 'You didn't just *find* that smoke machine at the committee meeting, did you?'

Tina's eyes widened. 'N-n-no....Santana gave it to me.'

'And you didn't think that was weird?' Rachel threw her hands in the air. How could Tina be so trusting? Didn't she know that the McKinley High student body was so socially stratified that someone from the upper echelon would never deign to help one of the lower creatures, like a Glee kid? 'That one of the Cheerios *suddenly* cared about a Glee performance?'

'I didn't think about it, okay?' Tina stared at the toes of her black sneakers. 'I thought she was just being nice.'

'*Nice?*' Rachel shook her head furiously. 'Maybe if you weren't trying so hard to fit in with the brainless and unscrupulous Cheerios, we wouldn't be in this situation.'

'Hey, that's below the belt.' Artie spoke up, wheeling toward Rachel. 'You can't blame Tina for not knowing how devious the Cheerios could be.'

Rachel rolled her eyes. She felt as if the ground beneath her feet were starting to crumble away. 'Big surprise that *you're* defending her. Everyone knows you have a big fat crush on her.'

'That is way out of line, girl.' Mercedes jumped to her feet and walked threateningly toward Rachel. 'Didn't your daddies teach you any manners?'

'You're just jealous of my talent.' Rachel felt like her back was against the wall, and she couldn't let the others keep putting her down. Everyone blamed her, and it wasn't fair. 'You have been since the moment I walked in that door.'

'Oh my God.' Mercedes sat back down in her chair. She

covered her eyes with her hands. Maybe if she couldn't see Rachel, she wouldn't feel the urge to strangle her. 'What planet are we standing on? Did she really just say that to me?'

'I think she did.' Kurt crossed his arms over his chest.

'Look, you're all mad at me for telling it like it is.' Rachel eyed each of them in turn. 'But basically, Cher was totally right. If you're not prepared to fail, you shouldn't be a performer.' She shook her head, suddenly sad. 'And you're not performers. You all care too much about what other people think. Which is just a stupid way to live your lives.' She was about to quote Olivia Newton-John, but she realized it wouldn't make any difference. 'It doesn't matter. I won't taint your little Glee Club with my presence anymore. I'm applying to performing arts schools, and I don't need any of you.' With that, she spun dramatically on her heel and stomped out of the room. If there was one thing Rachel knew how to do, it was make an exit.

Because it was homecoming week, each school day had a different theme. Monday was Seventies Day, and she passed a gaggle of Cheerios wearing bell-bottoms, peasant blouses, and obscenely short minidresses. They snickered as they passed Rachel. 'Nice singing, loser,' one of them spat out.

She marched to the guidance counselor's office, more determined than ever. This time she was not taking no for an answer.

'Miss Pillsbury?' Rachel spotted Miss Pillsbury in the hallway, wearing a pair of baby blue rubber gloves. She was scraping at a piece of gum that someone had stuck to the glass wall between her office and the hallway. 'I'm ready for the transfer applications now.'

'Rachel, are you sure?' Miss Pillsbury removed the piece of gum and carried it, on the scraper she kept just for that purpose, to the trash can. Now she needed to Windex the smudge it had left behind, but Rachel was standing there so expectantly. The counselor knew it was her duty to try to talk this girl down from the ledge, but she couldn't muster up the energy, not with that smudge on the glass.

'One hundred and ten percent.'

Miss Pillsbury sighed slightly and headed into her office. Gloves still on, she grabbed a sheaf of papers from a file holder on her shelf and handed them to Rachel. 'It looks like most of these are due soon, if you'd like to make the transfer this semester.' Miss Pillsbury grabbed her Windex bottle with a twinge of guilt. 'If you'd like to talk about it more, please do stop by later.'

'Thank you.' Rachel clutched the papers to her chest like a life preserver as she made her way to her locker through the rapidly filling hallways. One of these applications was her ticket out of here, and it was about time she used it. She watched as a guy in a letterman's jacket slammed a shorter guy into a wall of open lockers and then sipped his slushie as if nothing had happened. She didn't doubt that every school had its social hierarchies, but none could be as moronic as McKinley's. If only it were based on real talent – Rachel would immediately reign as queen.

Then she saw him. Finn. He was leaning against his locker, holding a thick math book in one hand. His hair was still wet from the shower, and he wore a gray T-shirt that was starting to fray around the neck.

Rachel stopped walking. Just at that moment, Finn looked up. He saw her and flashed a quick smile before turning and walking away.

In her post-performance fury, she'd forgotten about Finn. Leaving McKinley would mean giving up any chance she had with him. Even if the odds were against her ever knowing what it was like to kiss him, they would be nil if she transferred to a different school. But transferring could be her only shot at a future as a singer. Everyone knew the high school years were the formative years; did she really want to waste away at McKinley when she could be developing her talent?

But what if wasting away at McKinley gave her the only chance at Finn?

Her brain started whirling. Maybe it didn't have to be over for Glee Club. If there was a way to keep it alive – to make it better, stronger – and make everyone at McKinley see how good the group could be, then maybe she could stay.

A germ of an idea popped into her brain. The homecoming dance. The entire school would be in the gymnasium. Ready to be wowed.

But she couldn't do it alone. She was going to need the other Glee kids' help, which might be hard to get, as they all hated her now.

But she wouldn't be Rachel Berry if she gave up when faced with a challenge, no matter how insurmountable.

nineteen

Football practice, Tuesday after school

'**C**ome on, Brit. You're looking geriatric today. I've got soiled delicates that are fresher than your moves,' Coach Sylvester called through her white plastic megaphone. 'All right, none of you have earned a break, but if I don't give you all one, Social Services will come knocking again, and I don't need to be subjected to any more Kmart pantsuits. Take five.' She shook her head in disgust. Coach Sylvester was always extra demanding during the week before the homecoming game. The McKinley High football team was notoriously bad, and Coach Sylvester liked to remind the Cheerios that they were the real stars.

Quinn didn't care about Coach Sylvester's tough-love insults. She knew she'd been looking good. Great, even. It was because she was furious, and her anger was like rocket fuel to her backflips.

She grabbed her towel from the bench and dabbed at her neck. She'd been watching Puck across the field the whole time, which just made her angrier and even more powerful as she flung her body through the air. All week she'd been waiting for a follow-up to their conversation in the janitor's closet. But he never tried to get alone with her again, leaving Quinn feeling strangely rejected. Even though she knew it was a stupid game between them, she wasn't so ready for it to be over.

Yes, she'd told him it was over, but she hadn't exactly expected him to give up so quickly. Had she really been just a passing fancy? Had Puck just been after her because she was Quinn Fabray, president of the Celibacy Club, and he thought it would be funny to see if he could get in her pants? The thought made her blood boil.

Across the field, she could see Puck's group finish some kind of drill. Football looked so easy compared to cheering. The football players ran around a giant field trying to catch a big ball or trying to stop people from catching it, and they wore big thick pads the whole time, as if they were babies. The Cheerios, in contrast, worked every muscle in their bodies as they launched themselves through the air. Their timing had to be perfect – if it wasn't, the whole pyramid could come down. She'd like to see those football players try to stand on each other's shoulders and keep a smile on their faces.

Before she knew what she was doing, Quinn was halfway across the field to the football bench. Toward Puck. She could see Finn – as the tallest guy in school, he was easy to spot – near the end zone. He was busy running plays with his wide receivers, loudly calling out numbers, and she felt a wave of tenderness for him. She knew how important the homecoming game was to him.

'Congratulations.' Puck's back was to Quinn, and she leaned forward and said the word loudly in his ear.

He turned around and grinned at the sight of her standing behind the bench in her Cheerios uniform. In any other context, such a short skirt on a girl would mean she was a slut, but because it was a uniform, it somehow came off as wholesome and old-fashioned. And hot. Quinn's hair was pulled back into a ponytail, as it always was for practice, letting her sexy little ears stand out. Puck wished he could put one in his mouth and suck on it like a lollipop.

'On what? Did you see that tackle?' He squinted into the sunlight.

'No, I meant congratulations on going to the homecoming dance with Santana.' Quinn's voice was clipped, as if she was trying to keep her temper under control. 'You guys will make a really adorable couple.'

Puck wiped the sweat off his forehead with someone else's T-shirt. 'You heard about that already?'

'Of course I did. Santana wouldn't shut up about it all through practice.' Quinn flicked her ponytail over her shoulder. Santana had rushed up to Quinn in the girls' locker room before practice and thrown her arms around her friend, even though Quinn had just taken off her shirt and was standing there in her sports bra. 'He asked me!' Santana had squealed, and Quinn was happy for her for a second – before she realized that Santana meant *Puck* had asked her. A satisfied grin had stayed on Santana's face all through practice, and every time they got a break, she'd say something to Quinn like, 'I bet he's a great kisser' or 'I wonder if Puck'll bring me flowers.'

'Hey, you're not really mad at me? Because I'm going to the dance?' Puck stared at Quinn. Her cheeks were bright red, either from practice or because she'd gotten all hot and bothered over him. Which, he had to say, he liked. Maybe she was having second thoughts about her decision to wait around for clueless Finn to get the guts up to ask her.

'I thought you said you couldn't stand Santana,' Quinn hissed. A couple of players grabbed water from the bench and looked curiously at Quinn. 'You said her voice made your brain want to explode.'

'But she's hot.' Puck shrugged, grabbing his helmet from the bench. 'And available.'

'I can't believe you.' Quinn tried to look away, but his dark brown eyes had caught her. She felt the familiar flip-flop in the bottom of her belly – a feeling she never got around Finn, no matter how much she wished she did. Some things you couldn't fake.

'I can't believe you,' Puck shot back. 'In case you don't remember, I asked *you* to go to the dance with me. And you turned me down, remember?'

Quinn felt the anger rising in her. She'd always had a little problem with her temper. Once, in ninth grade, Mindy Johannes had accidentally let a drop of nail polish fall on Quinn's Cheerios uniform when she was doing her nails before a game, and Quinn had grabbed the bottle of Petal Pink and poured the whole thing in Mindy's faux Gucci purse. She hadn't meant to – she hadn't even thought about it while she was doing it. And now she felt the same way. It didn't matter how reasonable Puck was being – that just made it worse. Of course he was right. This whole thing was of Quinn's own making.

But it didn't stop her from wanting to hit him. To smack that smirk off his face. And then maybe kiss it.

'Remember?' Puck asked, stepping closer. Quinn closed her eyes. The memory of the janitor's closet came rushing back to her. Even the smell of floor polish seemed sexy when it involved Puck. This was it, she thought. This was the moment when she would let Puck kiss her in public. In front of the entire football team, all the Cheerios, the whole world. Finn would find out, and maybe he could take Santana to the dance, as a consolation prize, while Puck and Quinn slow danced on the gym floor.

'What's up, guys?'

Quinn's eyes flew open. Finn had appeared between them,

slapping Puck's back. His face seemed so innocent and honest, and she felt a stab of guilt. Then he focused on Quinn. 'I saw you standing over here. Are you done with practice?'

Quinn forced herself to focus on Finn. Puck could eat his heart out. 'No, just on break.' Boldly, she touched Finn's back. 'You looked good out there.'

Finn grinned sheepishly. He was the kind of guy who smiled with his whole face, not just his lips. He was a good guy, Quinn reminded herself. She wanted a good guy, didn't she? 'Listen, I've been meaning to ask you,' Finn started, then stopped. 'Do you...do you want to go to the homecoming dance? I mean, with me?'

Quinn smiled. It was happening. This was what she'd been waiting for. Still, she couldn't help glancing over at Puck, who had one foot on the bench and was leaning forward to stretch out his hamstrings. 'Yes, of course. I'd love to go with you, Finn.'

Puck didn't even flinch. 'Cool,' Finn said. 'I'd like to pick you up in my mom's car, but I think all the guys just get ready in the locker room after the game.'

'That's okay.' Quinn twirled a lock of her hair around her finger. 'I'm going over to Brit's to get ready.'

'Cool,' Finn repeated. 'So I'll meet you in the gym? At, like, nine?'

'That sounds perfect,' Quinn purred. Still no reaction from Puck. How could he be so unfazed? 'You know what else would be perfect? If we went in my parents' hot tub after

162

the dance. Maybe sneak some wine coolers.' Quinn couldn't believe what she was saying. She was never that suggestive. Boys had dirty-enough minds, as it was – it was the girl's job to keep them in line. And here she was, practically throwing herself at Finn.

But it was worth it. She saw Puck look up from his stretch. He looked pissed. Like he wanted to punch something – someone – in the face.

'That sounds awesome.' Finn was, understandably, psyched. Quinn Fabray, inviting him to a hot tub? The dance would be awesome, but the hot tub...even more awesome.

'Good.' Coach Sylvester's whistle blew, and Quinn started walking backward across the grass. She waved her fingers at Finn, ignoring Puck completely. 'Gotta get back to work now.' As she turned her back on the boys, she felt both Puck and Finn staring after her.

She had them both exactly where she wanted them. Puck might be going to the dance with Santana, but he'd be thinking of Quinn.

twenty

McKinley High hallway, Wednesday morning

'Care to get a refreshment?' Kurt asked as he sidled up to Mercedes's open locker. She was putting on grape-flavored lip gloss as she looked into her small locker mirror. 'I didn't get enough beauty sleep last night.'

Mercedes glanced at her phone for the time. 'God bless Mr Horn.' They had first period with the notoriously laid-back teacher. He'd smoked so much marijuana in the seventies that he regularly spaced out in class and let the kids come and go, as long as they promised to do so 'peacefully'. He had one of those construction-paper chains hanging behind his desk, the links representing the days left until his retirement, and he tore off one each day and tossed it into the trash. He'd been elected Teacher of the Year four times in a row.

'I need a caffeine pick-me-up.' Kurt checked his reflection in the glass wall of the guidance counselor's office as they walked past. He fixed his hair. 'My mojo has been seriously compromised.'

'Mine, too. Seriously.'

'Nice job in the show!' A thick-necked football player gave Kurt a good-natured shoulder in the chest, slamming him into a row of lockers. 'You guys rocked.'

'Thanks,' Kurt muttered, dusting himself off. He was annoyed at Rachel for giving them yet another reason to be mocked. 'I preferred it when they just trashed me without reason. I hate that they have something specific to hate me for.'

Mercedes smoothed Kurt's collar for him. 'Isn't there anything else for people to talk about? It's not like we're that interesting.'

'I don't know. I have a feeling that while we tend to fly under the radar with our nerdiness, Rachel's presence in Glee happened to bring it all to the forefront.' It was true. Rachel seemed to strike a chord with everyone.

'I knew this would happen.' Mercedes stopped short of saying 'I told you so,' but she meant it. 'Rachel's just a diva who never cared about any of us.'

They arrived at the snack bar, a portion of the cafeteria that was open throughout the day for quick shots of sugar and caffeine. Public-school food reform movements that called for fewer sugary and processed foods were ignored in

Lima, where the student population was firmly attached to the slushie (unfortunate for nerds).

Kurt nodded slowly as he stepped past the slushie machine – whirring ominously – and the towering stack of plastic cups next to it. 'Maybe it was a mistake to invite her into the club. She drove everybody completely insane.'

Still, he felt guilty about the whole thing. Rachel had been his idea, and he wasn't totally convinced he'd been wrong. When he was a kid, he'd gone away to New York to a tennis camp; his father had wanted to foster some sort of athletic ability in his son, and Kurt had expressed an interest in tennis after seeing old photos of tennis players in their short tennis whites. His instructor, a tall teenage boy named Stefan with golden hair and a backhand like an ocean wave, had insisted he play with boys above his skill level. 'It's the fastest way to improve,' Stefan had said as he stretched his racket into the air and smashed the ball across the net. Kurt could have happily watched him play all day. In any case, Rachel did make the others want to be better. 'But I still think...'

'No.' Mercedes was adamant. She leaned over to examine a blueberry muffin wrapped in cellophane. 'It's over.'

'Good morning, McKinley High!' There was a moment of static before Rachel's voice came over the loudspeakers.

'Speak of the devil, and the devil appears,' Mercedes whispered, making a spooky gesture with her fingertips.

Kurt grabbed a plastic cup. It had a drawing of a plastic cup on it, which Kurt always found bizarrely meta. He knew

167

it was a cup. That's why he was using it for a drink in the first place.

Rachel's voice continued over the loudspeaker. 'Congratulations to the girls' soccer team for crushing the Maryvale Flyers in a five-one blowout. Reminder to the French Club members that there's a meeting in Madame Smith's room after school. She will provide the baguettes and *chocolat*.'

Mercedes rolled her eyes as Rachel burst into a song called 'Wednesday Week' by Elvis Costello. Where did she get her terrible taste in music? The last thing Mercedes wanted to do was listen to Rachel rattle on. It was cruel and unusual punishment. Maybe she'd start a protest letter to Principal Figgins during Mr Horn's class today. Even Mrs Applethorpe was better than Rachel.

'Now, I have something personal to say,' Rachel's disembodied voice announced.

'That girl is too much.' Mercedes placed her hands over her ears.

'If she says something about her period, I'm going to pass out,' Kurt said as he pushed the DIET COLA button on the giant black machine that spewed out generic sodas. The cold carbonated liquid sprayed into his cup.

'I just would like to take this time to apologize to the Glee kids. I was wrong. I'd like to award you all Rachel Berry's Gold Stars of the Week for being talented singers and good human beings.'

Mercedes tugged at her earlobe as if something was wrong with her hearing. 'Did she just say what I think she said?'

Kurt nodded in shock. 'I heard it, too.' He had thought Rachel Berry was the kind of girl who never admitted she was wrong. He could picture her picking fights over answers on Trivial Pursuit cards and asserting that she was smarter than the board game creators.

Rachel continued. 'I hope we can all get over our creative differences in the future, and I hope to see you all at the homecoming dance. Have a happy Wednesday, everyone.'

Kurt and Mercedes stared at each other. 'That was uncharacteristically kind of Rachel,' Kurt said as he pulled a five-dollar bill from his pocket.

'I know. It's weird. She's so self-involved, I didn't think she was capable of realizing she'd hurt anyone else's feelings,' Mercedes said.

Kurt stuffed the change into a pocket of his leather messenger bag. 'Are you also reconsidering your stance on the homecoming dance?' he asked as they stepped back into the hallway.

Mercedes stopped unwrapping the plastic from her blueberry muffin. Her heart beat faster. 'Why? Are you?'

Kurt shrugged casually. 'Maybe. That is, if you'd be willing to accompany me.' He could already picture himself walking into the gymnasium in his gorgeous gray Tom Ford suit. Everyone's eyes would fall on him, wondering where he got such exquisite taste. His shoes! He needed to find a pair of shoes that lived up to the suit. Mall today.

'Okay.' Mercedes tried to sound casual, but she could feel the excitement building in her throat. Kurt just asked her to the dance. It was incredible. He liked her! Now she just needed to find something to wear. 'It's a date.'

Maybe one of Rachel's plans could have a positive result, after all.

twenty-one

McKinley High gym, Thursday after school

Thursday after school, the decorations committee had its second and final meeting in the gym. The Cheerios and the wannabes had been rushing around the gym for twenty minutes, putting together their assignments – and things looked terrible. The gym looked exactly like a gym. Someone had hung gold tinsel around the rim of the basketball nets, which just made them look like toilets with those puffy seat cushions that grandmothers always had in their houses. Someone else – Brittany, perhaps – had stuck giant cutout letters spelling HOMCOMING on the mats against the wall. A random papier-mâché palm tree stood in one corner.

'This looks terrible,' Santana Lopez announced mournfully.

She hadn't had time to do her part, through no fault of her own. First, she'd been anxiously wondering whether Puck was going to ask her to the dance. She hadn't even been able to eat anything besides French fries, she'd been so upset. Then, after he finally asked her, she had so much to think about – which dress to buy, which earrings to shoplift from Macy's, which bra-and-panties set to wear. She'd completely blown off the decorations project, hoping that everyone else would just pick up the slack.

But everyone else had been equally distracted, and consequently nothing substantial had been done to disguise the gym's gym-ness. Kirsten Niedenhoffer pressed her fingers to her temples as if she felt a migraine coming on. 'Who was in charge of the coronation stage?' she demanded. A low platform at one end of the auditorium had been trimmed with gold tinsel. At the back of the platform stood a curved white arbor that probably had been filched from someone's garden. 'It looks like it belongs at a low-budget wedding.'

The girls stared at one another uncomfortably, and one of them spoke up. 'I'm really sorry, but Coach Sylvester was riding us all so hard this week, we just didn't have the energy to do anything else.'

'And we were all busy selling votes for homecoming king and queen.' A girl named Annie stared longingly at the stage. 'It was hard work.'

'I bought a hot-pink minidress with a black lace bustier, and it's going to look really awful with these crappy decorations,' Brittany whined. 'They're going to make the dress look cheap.'

'That *dress* makes the dress look cheap,' someone whispered, but Brittany didn't hear.

'What are we going to do?' Santana demanded. It wasn't fair that her first date with Puck was going to be in the lame school gym. It was so unromantic. She'd been planning on hooking up with him in the backseat of his car, but how was she supposed to get in the mood when the gym looked more like a place to play dodgeball than the magical wonderland it was supposed to be?

As if in reply, Tina appeared in the doorway, wearing a gray-and-black-striped off-the-shoulder T-shirt over a pair of black leggings. With one arm she pressed an overstuffed black trash bag to her chest; with the other she dragged an equally giant bag behind her on the ground. The bag made a shuffling sound against the hardwood floors, and everyone turned to stare at her.

'Who let the bag lady onto school property?' Santana asked, sending the other girls into fits of giggles. Really, they never should have let someone like that Tina girl come to the meeting in the first place. She'd probably got slushied in the hallway and was now going to do some crazy *Carrie* thing and throw tampons all over the gym.

'Did you bring some trash to decorate with?' Kirsten asked as Tina approached. 'Is that how you do things in your house?'

'It's not t-t-trash.' Tina carefully set the black trash bags

173

on the floor and opened one. Curious, the girls on the bleachers leaned forward to peer in. Inside were dozens – no, hundreds – of gorgeous, glittery gold stars. 'I just took some things home and worked on them.'

Santana's jaw dropped practically to the floor. 'These are amazing.' She snatched a star from the top of the pile. 'What did you do?'

Tina shrugged. 'I just took the old stars and spray-painted them with fresh gold paint that had a shimmer to it.' She picked up a star and held it by the clear plastic string attached to the top point. 'I thought I saw some wire in the decorations boxes. We could string it across the gym like clotheslines and dangle the stars from it.'

Everyone pictured the gymnasium darkened and filled with sparkling stars that dangled over their heads as they slow danced. 'That would look really gorgeous,' Kirsten admitted.

'I know,' Tina said with uncharacteristic confidence. A couple of girls were tearing through the bags, separating the stars by size. Tina turned to face Santana. 'By the way, your little prank with the smoke machine was really low. We were just trying to perform.'

Santana narrowed her eyes. 'Is that what this is about, then? Are these stars doused in arsenic or something?'

Tina rolled her eyes. 'No, I just worked on these stars to show you what it means to be above all that.' She smirked. 'Besides, unless you're planning on licking them, arsenic wouldn't do much.'

Kirsten sniffed at the star she was holding. It didn't smell poisoned. 'That's really big of you,' she said with only a touch of sarcasm. While she couldn't let this Goth loser girl totally insult her social betters, Kirsten knew the committee needed these stars for the dance. The palm tree in the corner was not cutting it.

'Besides,' Tina said, with her hands on her hips, 'you guys have no artistic skills *whatsoever*. And you spelled *homecoming* wrong again.' Tina smiled proudly at everyone. She hadn't smiled like that since she got braces, in the seventh grade.

Once again, jaws were on the floor. Tina felt a rush of pride in herself. This time she'd stood up to the Cheerios, and she hadn't even stuttered. And now...everyone was staring at her, waiting for further instructions. From *her*. 'Why don't you set up those ladders and start stringing the wires across the gym? I've got another two bags of stars in my car.'

Tina left the auditorium with her whole body tingling. She'd done it! She'd told the Cheerios what to do, and they were doing it. She had to tell Artie. He had stayed late after school to work on the newspaper – he was writing an exposé on school elevator access. Instead of going out to the parking lot, Tina headed to the newspaper room.

Through the glass-windowed door of the paper room, she spotted Artie sitting in front of a computer, typing away. She thumped her fist on the glass, and Artie glanced up at the noise. In his argyle sweater-vest and short-sleeved button-down,

175

he looked so cute. His shaggy brown hair was in dire need of a haircut. He wheeled himself to the door.

'Hey,' he said, opening the door and wheeling into the hallway. 'I thought you were decorating the gym.'

'I had to get another bag of stars from my car.' Tina felt her face flush. She was a little embarrassed that she'd rushed all the way here just to tell Artie about what had happened.

'Did they like them?' Artie asked. When he'd talked to Tina in eighth-period precalculus, she said she was nervous about showing up at the committee meeting. He made fists with his hands and mock-punched the air. 'Did you show them what's what?'

Tina smiled. 'Sort of. I showed them my decorations, and they almost passed out.' She grinned at the memory. 'And then I t-t-told them that theirs sucked and that their prank was lame. And then I bossed them around.'

'That's awesome.' Artie was really proud of her. Tina was one of the coolest people he knew, and it made him sad to see her letting people push her around. 'I wish I'd been there to see the looks on their faces.'

'At least you can see the decorations.' She looked at him shyly. 'I mean, if you go to the dance.'

'I think Rachel was right.' Artie tapped his fingers against his wheels. 'I mean, when she said we shouldn't let the popular kids tell us where we can and can't go.'

'You want to go?'

'Definitely.' Artie suddenly felt nervous. He was actually

going to a school dance? He wondered what Tina would wear – something black, no doubt, and really pretty. He didn't want Tina to leave yet. 'What about Rachel? Do you buy her apology?'

Tina chewed on the inside of her cheek. 'Yeah. I think, maybe, she's not as b-b-bad as she comes off.'

'I guess the worst that she did was have faith in us,' Artie said, staring at the floor. 'That's not so bad.'

Tina smiled shyly. 'I think we can probably forgive her.'

'Nerds need to stick together.'

She didn't even mind being called a nerd by Artie. He made it sound like a compliment.

twenty-two

Quinn's house, Thursday night

'It's lovely, darling,' Quinn's mother, Judy, said, touching Quinn's homecoming dress with the hand that wasn't holding her before-bedtime glass of pinot noir. The dress was on a hanger tucked over the door of Quinn's closet, and the two of them had bought it over the weekend at a small boutique in Dayton, even before Quinn knew she was going to the dance with Finn. 'It reminds me of the dress I wore to cotillion. Back when I was your size.'

Quinn stared at the dress from where she was sitting at her vanity. It *was* lovely. It was an empire-waisted dress in a delicate buttercream yellow, with a sweetheart neckline and a chiffon skirt that flared out and ended just above her knees. It was ultrafeminine and classy, but there was something about it that was undeniably sexy. Quinn Fabray had mastered the art of looking wholesome while also driving the boys wild. The slender spaghetti straps, made of a pale yellow ribbon, looked innocently seductive against her bare skin. She knew, just looking at the dress, that it was perfect. Most of the girls at McKinley tended to overstate their sex appeal with dresses that were too short and promised too much. Quinn, though, knew that the way to really make the boys ache was to look as pure as possible – so they could wonder what it would take to corrupt you. The dress, she knew, would drive Puck crazy.

Except she was going to the dance with Finn.

'Tell me about this Finn boy, sweetheart.' Quinn's mother sank down on the edge of Quinn's queen-size bed. She pushed aside the stuffed teddy bear that Quinn slept with. 'Will your father like him?'

Quinn turned on her vanity stool and stared at her reflection in the mirror. 'Does Daddy like *anyone*?' Quinn asked, watching her mother in the background. Her father tolerated boyfriends but never really 'liked' them. He'd only started calling her older sister Frannie's boyfriend by his first name when they got engaged. Finn, a tall, handsome quarterback, would definitely be tolerated by her father. Even though Finn was a little weird sometimes, and talked to the school nerds and losers a little more than was strictly necessary, he was superficially the kind of guy her father could reluctantly give his approval to.

180

Puck, with his Mohawk, torn jeans, and a cocky attitude written all over his face, wouldn't get past the front door of the Fabrays' Tudor mansion. His face had DANGER written all over it, and Mr Fabray would take one look at him and call the cops.

'He loves *you*, sweetheart.' Quinn's mother stood up and walked over to Quinn, her heels – which she wore at all times – wobbling in Quinn's thick, cream-colored carpet. 'He just wants you to be happy.'

'I know.' Quinn looked at her own face in the mirror for so long that it no longer seemed like her own. Her honey-blond hair was still sun-streaked from a summer of tennis lessons at the country club and afternoons at the town pool, where all the cute boys hung out to do laps. She tried to picture this girl being crowned homecoming queen in a pretty buttercream dress that set off her tan. That's what she wanted. To be onstage, next to Finn, her handsome counterpart. 'I am. Happy, I mean.'

'Good.' Her mother kissed Quinn on the back of the head. 'You'll make a beautiful homecoming queen.' Quinn watched her mom's reflection as she disappeared out the door.

Quinn turned up the Lady Gaga song on her iPod so that she could listen while she brushed her teeth. She felt sorry for any teenage girl who grew up without her own personal bathroom. No one ever told her she was taking too long in the shower, or got annoyed when she took a luxurious bubble bath. But sometimes her big bedroom and her big bathroom felt lonely. She considered calling Santana but realized she couldn't listen to any more of the girl's plans for how far she was going to let Puck get.

Quinn halfheartedly did her facial routine with the über-expensive Swedish facial products her mother imported because they hadn't been officially approved by the FDA. Her mother was always pointing out that the time to do something about wrinkles was before they showed up.

As Quinn brushed her teeth, she tried to picture being crowned homecoming queen tomorrow. She was a shoo-in – some of the Cheerios had already looked at the votes and had said there was no competition. And Finn would be there with her. Perfect. She'd got a pair of silver strappy sandals with three-inch heels, higher than she normally wore, just so she wouldn't look silly next to him onstage.

As she slipped into her white satin pajamas, she couldn't help wondering what it would feel like to slow dance with Puck's warm, strong hands on her hips. She lifted her thick down comforter and climbed into bed, letting herself imagine going to the dance with Puck. People would be shocked to see Quinn with a guy who had a reputation like Puck's. Even if nothing happened between them, the rumors would fly. Quinn would never be the pure golden girl again.

But her face felt hot just thinking about him in a suit.

Just as she was about to drift off, her phone buzzed on her nightstand. She lifted up her silk sleeping mask and stared. *Look outside*, the text message said. It was from Puck's number.

Was she dreaming? Quinn sat up straight in bed. She kind of hoped she was dreaming. She threw off the covers and opened her curtains. On the street, just past her driveway, half-hidden by the hundred-year-old oak trees that lined the Fabrays' front yard, was a black Chevy Suburban.

Quinn took a deep breath. What did Puck think he was doing? If her father saw a teenager with a Mohawk lurking in front of their house, she'd be lucky if he just called the police. Puck had to get out of there.

Quickly, heart thumping against her ribs, Quinn stepped into a pair of soft black ballet flats and opened the door to her bedroom. Down the hall, the door to her parents' room was closed, and she could hear the sounds of Jay Leno doing his monologue. And her father's deep snores. Perfect. She crept down the back staircase, not even sure why she was being so quiet. She was just going downstairs, after all. She couldn't sleep and needed a glass of skim milk, if anyone asked.

Quinn was surprised at how easy it was to just walk out of her house. When she stepped outside, she was again surprised, this time by the brightness of the moon. Crickets chirped loudly from the bushes. It was cool, but not cold, outside, and the air smelled startlingly fresh. Her shoes made almost no sound against the blacktop as she marched to the end of the driveway. She pulled open the Suburban's passenger door and slid into the seat. 'What the hell are you doing here?' she hissed, sounding angrier than she really felt. In fact, she wasn't angry at all.

Puck seemed to know that. He moistened his lips as he leaned against the door and looked at Quinn. 'You didn't text back. I didn't think you were coming.'

'Then why didn't you leave?' she asked. The inside of the car smelled slightly of smoke and Febreze. An old Neil Diamond song was playing on the radio. The car was surprisingly neat – she had expected to find fast-food wrappers and Red Bull cans. 'And what are you listening to?'

'Sorry.' Puck changed to a different station. A Billy Joel song came on, which was slightly better. 'Nice jammies.' He touched Quinn's knee.

She felt as if she'd been electrocuted. Maybe it was the satin pajamas. But when she walked around in them on the carpeted floors and touched her cat, Miss Cleo, she didn't give off shocks. She shifted away from him. 'Seriously, Puck. What are you doing here?' She brushed her hair off her face. 'What do you think would happen if my father found out? Or if Finn did?' That thought gave her a different kind of chill. She didn't want to hurt Finn, no matter what.

'I just wanted to talk.' He was wearing a black V-neck T-shirt with two gray stripes down the sides, and he looked as though he'd shaved for the occasion. His chin was baby-soft and looked kissable.

Quinn felt herself falling over the edge again. She rubbed her hands up and down her arms, even though she wasn't cold. In fact, it felt really warm in the truck. Or maybe it was just being in such close quarters with Puck again. She tried

184

not to think about what had happened last time. 'Yeah, I've heard that line before.'

'Can I help it if you're insanely attracted to me?' Puck smiled at her. He had the longest lashes she'd ever seen on a guy. The windows of the Suburban were slowly starting to fog up from their breath.

Quinn's hand went to the door, but Puck leaned over and grabbed her arm. 'Don't go. I was just kidding.'

'Then talk.' Quinn tried not to meet Puck's eyes. It was too easy to get stuck in them. It was like he was some crazy hypnotist, and all he needed to do was get her into an enclosed area and stare soulfully into her eyes, and she would go as limp as a kitten. She stared at his forehead instead. What the hell was going on with him? Or with her? She was so used to being the one in control with boys. She *liked* saying no to guys. It came naturally to her, and it was extremely satisfying.

Puck cleared his throat. 'I want to come clean to Finn.'

Quinn's hazel eyes widened. 'About what?'

'About this. About us.' Puck had prepared a speech on his way over, but he was having trouble thinking straight with Quinn so close to him. And in her sexy white silky pajamas, like those a rich lady who lived in a hotel would wear. Her face was completely makeup-less, and she smelled like pears and toothpaste. 'Come to the dance with me. I'm a way better dancer than Finn, anyway.'

Quinn stared out the windshield of the car. It was the only way she wouldn't melt at Puck's words. She could see her neighbor Mr Lipanski's mailbox, and she wondered what would happen if he were to take his Boston terrier, Winston, out for a late walk and see Quinn sitting in the street with a strange guy. Would he say something to her father? Probably not. She sensed that Mr Lipanski didn't like her father.

'I can't go with you.' Her eyes focused on Mr Lipanski's front porch light. 'You're going with Santana, remember?'

'I'll bail on her.' A lock of Quinn's hair had fallen in front of her face like a curtain, hiding her expression from Puck. With his thumb, he brushed the hair back behind her ear. His hand lingered at her neck.

'She's my friend. I could never do that to her.' Quinn closed her eyes. Her voice sounded funny, even to her. A Journey song came on the radio next, and neither of them moved to change the station. Puck was running his thumb across her jaw now, and it felt so good that she couldn't push him away. Not yet. 'Or to Finn. He's a good guy.' He smelled like shaving cream.

'We've got to do something,' Puck said, inhaling the scent of Quinn's hair. 'I can't stand this.'

Quinn found herself reaching for Puck's hand. Part of her wanted to ask him to pray with her. That's what the pastor's wife taught the girls in the youth group to do when they felt like things were moving too fast. Puck hadn't even kissed her yet, though. 'Can't stand what?'

Puck touched his nose to her cheek. 'Not being with you.

It's driving me crazy.' His voice was throaty and warm in her ear. The tiny hairs on the back of her neck stood on end.

Quinn knew it was time to go back to her room. She needed to get out of the car now, sneak back into the house, pour herself a glass of milk, and go to bed. Forget that all this with Puck had happened. Maybe she could convince herself it was all a dream. It felt like a dream – like one she'd been having since she first started thinking of Puck this way.

She pushed Puck away. 'There's nothing we can do. There's just no way it can work out.'

Puck rubbed his hands over his eyes wearily. If he had said something – anything – the spell might have been broken. But he just sat there, staring at the car radio, listening to the Journey song. He didn't move away from Quinn, and she could feel the heat from his body next to hers. Why did guys always give off so much heat? Was it all their testosterone?

She knew it was a mistake before she said it, but she couldn't imagine sneaking back into her house right now, back up the stairs to her quiet bedroom, to sleep in her giant empty bed. Not when Puck was right next to her, giving off enough heat to start a bonfire.

And she knew it was a mistake as she was saying it, but she couldn't make the words stop as they tumbled out of her mouth. It was true that it would never work out with Puck, for a million different reasons. But it was also true that she couldn't imagine getting out of his car without once again feeling his lips on hers.

'How about one last kiss, for good measure?' she asked, finally meeting his eyes.

Almost before she had finished the sentence, he kissed her. One of his hands slid to the nape of her neck, pulling her toward him. She forgot about what the neighbors might see or what her parents might think or how Finn and Santana would feel if they knew what was going on right then.

Instead, she just thought about Puck. About how his hands and his lips felt against her body, and suddenly, everything else was easy.

twenty-three

McKinley High gym, Friday night, homecoming dance

To no one's surprise, the McKinley High football team lost to Central Valley at the Friday night homecoming game by a score of 18–6, but it didn't affect the students' spirits as they arrived at the gymnasium for the dance. The gym looked beautiful, like a starry wonderland. The lights were turned down low, and giant gold stars dangled from wire lines that stretched across the gym, their glitter sparkling as they turned and swayed, as if they were real stars blinking in the night sky. Music blared from the sound system, where a scruffy DJ presided over the stereo tables. All the students looked their best. The room was filled with boys in suits or blazers and girls wearing brightly colored dresses and high heels that clicked against the floor daintily. A few faculty chaperones clustered around the long cafeteria table under the basketball hoop, where punch and cookies were spread out on fancy trays.

Rachel Berry sat perched on the bleachers, waiting anxiously. She was wearing a teal blue strapless dress with a tiered skirt and a black sash around her waist. Her kitten-heeled open-toe black shoes tapped against the wood floor, revealing her nervousness. She'd arrived at the dance the moment it started, anxious to find out if her apology was enough and if the Glee kids would show up. She wanted her scheme to go off without a hitch, but it wasn't something she could do alone.

'You look enchanting this evening.' Jacob stood in front of Rachel. He was wearing a navy blue blazer and a pair of brown pressed pants that were an inch too short. A brown-and-pink paisley necktie was knotted too tight around his neck, and the pattern made Rachel think of the drawings of sperm in her health textbook.

'Thank you for the compliment, Jacob, but I'm not dancing with you again.' She had agreed to dance with him at last year's holiday ball, just because no one else had asked her, and Jacob's hands kept straying a little too far from the acceptable positions. 'Last time you groped me in the middle of the dance floor.' He'd also left sweaty palm prints on her dress, but she felt it would be a low blow to mention that.

'What if I promise to keep my hands above the equator this time?' Sweat beads were starting to form on his forehead.

'No,' Rachel insisted. There was some sort of commotion

190

at the door, and Rachel tried to see what was happening. The crowd parted, and Finn Hudson stepped through the doorway with Quinn Fabray on his arm. Rachel felt her breath catch in her throat. Finn was wearing a navy blue suit and a pale blue button-down. His tie had dark blue and yellow diagonal stripes. He looked incredibly handsome, all dressed up, and only slightly uncomfortable. Quinn, at his side, looked like a fairy princess in a pale, buttery yellow dress that matched Finn's tie. That tiny detail almost broke Rachel's heart. Quinn's blond hair fell around her shoulders in loose curls – perfect for placing a tiara on.

'If you've been following my blog, you've seen that exit polls practically confirmed that Finn Hudson and Quinn Fabray will be crowned king and queen tonight.' Jacob pushed his glasses up on his nose.

Rachel didn't need Jacob's stupid blog to tell her that. It was apparent from the way everyone stared at the golden couple, with envy in their eyes as Quinn tugged Finn by the hand and pulled him to the middle of the dance floor. Quinn had a Miss America–caliber smile plastered on her face, and she positively glowed from all the attention. Finn couldn't possibly truly like Quinn, could he? She *did* look amazing, but she was so bitchy and bossy.

Finn was so much deeper than that – or, at least, Rachel thought he was. Hoped he was.

While Rachel was watching Finn and Quinn dance, Artie and Tina came through the doorway, to much less fanfare.

Artie's father had picked Tina up in his handicapped-accessible van and driven the two of them to school, but she wasn't totally sure whether this qualified as a date. Artie had told her she looked pretty when she got into the car, but his dad was there, so it wasn't exactly romantic. She'd borrowed a dress from her sister – a black minidress with sheer, fluttery black sleeves – and had polished her knee-high Doc Martens until they shone.

'You did this?' Artie asked, staring up in awe at the field of stars over their heads. 'This looks totally amazing, like something out of a movie.'

Tina looked at all the stars. She'd made some small and medium-size ones and hung them randomly on the lines so that it looked like a bunch of stars had tumbled down to Earth. 'You really like it?'

'Are you kidding? You could be a set designer or something.' Artie straightened his tie. He felt a little funny in his black suit, as if he were going to a funeral. His mother had bought him a new Ralph Lauren royal blue dress shirt from the mall, where he never liked to go because people always looked at him like he was in the way. 'It's...magical.'

Tina flushed. She was really proud of how the gym had turned out, and it was nice to hear Artie's sweet words. She was about to say something – she'd forgotten to tell him that he looked nice, too, all dressed up – when Rachel rushed toward them, ruining the moment.

'Tina, the decorations are superb.' Rachel beamed at Artie

and Tina. She was just so glad to see them here. 'I'm flattered and honored that you chose my signature gold star to be the inspiration for the incredible job that you did.' She stopped talking abruptly. 'I mean, at least maybe in some part.'

Artie and Tina glanced at each other. It was impossible to stay angry with Rachel when she was just so clueless. 'Rachel, we agreed to forgive you, but don't push your luck,' Artie said.

'You guys are the best. And you both look really nice, too.' Rachel beamed again and glanced over her shoulder toward the stage. 'And I'm really glad you showed up, because I have a plan to make up for what happened at the assembly.'

'A p-p-plan?' Tina stuttered, suddenly nervous again. She was happy to be here at the big dance and watch everyone as they walked through the door and admired her stars. She didn't need anything more. Why did Rachel have to have so many plans?

'Yes.' Rachel recoiled slightly when a football player carrying a cup of punch walked toward her. It wasn't a slushie, but Rachel still didn't want it all over her dress. Fortunately, the guy handed the cup to his date instead of hurling it at Rachel. 'We are going to sing tonight, right here, for the whole student body.'

'Here?' Artie asked. He glanced around the crowded gym. 'How are we going to manage that?'

'I've figured it all out,' Rachel said. She pointed to the DJ booth. 'We just have to momentarily mess with the sound system and grab a few microphones.'

'I don't know if that's a great idea,' Tina said slowly. She liked to deliberate things carefully before making a decision, and this just seemed rushed. Like a disaster waiting to happen. What if this was yet another huge mistake? 'Haven't we m-m-mortified ourselves enough already?'

'Yes, and now it's our chance to make up for it.' Rachel's body hummed with excitement. She knew this plan would work. They should have done something like this in the first place, instead of trying to sing an old Broadway song that didn't really suit them. 'Tina, it's your night tonight. Your decorations look amazing, and the Cheerios all know that the only reason the dance looks nice at all is because of you.'

'That's true,' Artie agreed, turning to Tina. 'You do already have one victory over the Cheerios under your belt.'

'This is your chance.' Rachel glanced over her shoulder at Finn. Quinn's hand was on his shoulder, and her pink nails looked like talons to Rachel.

'I don't know.' Tina nodded toward the doorway. 'Let's see what they think.' Kurt and Mercedes had just walked in, looking fabulous. Kurt was wearing his new dark gray single-breasted Tom Ford suit with a white shirt and a thin black tie. He walked into the gym with the confidence of someone who knew he was the best-dressed person in the room. Curvy Mercedes knew she had to look extra good next to Kurt, so she'd borrowed her father's credit card and splurged on a dark purple bustier top, which highlighted her best features, and a slim black tulip skirt. A sparkling rhinestone headband held back her hair.

Rachel smiled to herself as she waved to Kurt and Mercedes. The two of them were divas, and she couldn't imagine them turning down the chance to perform again, especially when they were dressed to the nines. Things were definitely starting to come together for her.

Not everyone was so happy. Across the gym, Quinn Fabray was having a hard time keeping a smile on her face. Brittany lived just a few blocks from the school, and she had invited Quinn and Santana to get ready for the dance at her house after the game. Quinn had spent a torturous hour listening to Santana prattle on about how hot Puck was and how she didn't know if she'd be able to control herself around him. Quinn had wanted to puke.

She hadn't been able to think about anything but Puck. She'd hoped the other night would be the breaking point of the fever, and afterward she could go back to normal, but it hadn't worked out that way. She'd seen him in school on Friday, of course, but they didn't have a chance to say anything; they just shared charged little smiles.

But after watching Santana pour her thin, lithe body into a red backless minidress from Express, Quinn couldn't help hoping that Puck just wouldn't show up at the dance. No luck. When she and her sidekicks walked in the door, Puck,

Finn, and the other football guys were already there, having showered and dressed in the locker room.

'You look hot,' Puck had managed to whisper in Quinn's ear when Finn was getting her a plastic cup of punch, but she hadn't seen him and Santana since then. Santana was probably itching for the chance to lure Puck away from the crowd and jump on him, but she couldn't have done that already, could she? They were nowhere to be seen. Quinn tried not to imagine them in his car, fogging up the windows.

'Are you okay?' Finn asked, touching Quinn's bare arm. 'You look nervous.'

Quinn smiled up at him, trying to clear her head. She was here with Finn, not Puck, and she needed to focus on that. This was supposed to be *her* night. She was going to be crowned homecoming queen, and when Principal Figgins placed the crown on her head, everyone would clap and whisper about how pretty she was. 'I guess I'm just hoping we'll win king and queen.'

'Oh.' A glazed look passed over Finn's face. He was glad to be here with Quinn and all, and she looked really pretty with her hair down. But he couldn't make himself care about something as meaningless as winning homecoming king. He barely even cared about losing the football game, and that was more important to him. If he couldn't get a football scholarship, what was he supposed to do with his life? He looked down at Quinn, whose lips were glistening in the low lighting. It was kind of strange that she'd brought up the hot-tub thing the other day, but she hadn't mentioned it since then, so he didn't know whether the offer was for real.

'We should really mingle more,' Quinn said, grabbing Finn's arm. If she was going to be here with Finn, the least she could do was enjoy being the belle of the ball. Finn was one of the most popular guys in school, and she knew all the Cheerios were dying with jealousy that Quinn had snared him.

Besides, if she could focus on playing the part, maybe she'd start to forget about what she was missing.

'Let's go talk to Kirsten and her boyfriend. He's in college.'

Finn let himself get dragged away. His eyes started to glaze over, and he wished he were at home playing Halo. Then he caught sight of a girl in a greenish blue dress. Was that Rachel Berry? She had the sides of her long dark hair pulled back in one of those twist things that girls did, and she looked really pretty. He felt the urge to walk over to her and say something. He was really sorry the Cheerios had managed to pull off their stupid prank, and he felt bad that his warning hadn't been enough to protect her. He wasn't sure why he cared, but he felt like there was something more to Rachel than what everyone else saw.

'Hello?' Quinn tapped him on the arm. 'Are you coming?'

'Yeah,' he said. Rachel had disappeared into the crowd, and he felt a kind of funny feeling in his chest, like he'd just missed out on something.

twenty-four

McKinley High gym, homecoming dance, later

As Rachel had suspected, Mercedes and Kurt didn't need much coaxing to agree to her plan. 'Since my breakout performance left something to be desired, the idea of getting a second chance is rather appealing,' Kurt said, stroking the lapels of his jacket. 'Besides, how often do I look this good?'

'You always look good.' Mercedes patted his arm. She was in an incredible mood. She loved going to a social function with a date, for once. The gym looked really awesome, thanks to Tina. Mercedes was wearing new clothes, a pair of sexy purple platform shoes, and some serious bling – a giant rhinestone *M* pendant hanging around her neck, new gold hoop earrings, and a giant sparkling ring from Claire's boutique that Kurt told her looked 'smashing'. She felt like a rock star. And now she was going to get to perform? It was almost too good to be true. 'When do we get our chance?'

'Soon. Maybe after they do the boring coronation thing.' Rachel felt alive with excitement. This was it. She could feel it coming. 'I've got to scope out the DJ booth.' Her heels clicked against the floor as she made her way through the couples swaying to a Coldplay song. When she was halfway to the DJ booth, the song ended.

Everyone turned slightly toward the stage. People nudged each other as they watched Brittany totter up the steps in her silver stilettos. In her tight-fitting hot-pink-and-black mini and her hair pulled back into an upsweep, she looked like a Barbie doll.

Brittany approached the microphone. After a brief squeal of feedback, she started talking in a superfast voice that was almost impossible to understand. 'It's now time for the part of the evening you've all been waiting for, the crowning of the king and queen of the homecoming dance,' she read from an index card without taking a breath.

The room buzzed with excitement. As Rachel inched toward the DJ booth, she heard people whispering about Quinn and Finn and how they had to win. As she skirted the edge of the crowd, she passed Coach Sylvester talking to the mousy-looking economics teacher. 'It was a worthwhile investment,' Rachel overheard Coach Sylvester say. 'I was more than happy to pay for votes out of the school's arts program funding in order to maintain the delicate social structure that teenagers need to separate the weak from the strong.'

'Is that really fair?' Mrs Iggulden whispered back, sounding slightly aghast. Rachel stopped in her tracks, straining to hear every word.

'Using the funds? Sure.' Coach Sylvester was wearing a black tracksuit. 'The money goes straight back to the Cheerios' tanning fund, anyway. It's a win-win.'

Rachel's hands started to shake. She knew Coach Sylvester was shady, but this was egregious. She'd bought votes for the election? *Everything* was rigged – the homecoming race, the Fall in Love with Music recital. But instead of making her want to pull out her hair and transfer to another school, this time the wrongness of it inspired her. She was going to show them.

'And the winners are Quinn Fabray and Finn Hudson,' Brittany announced, forgetting to open the sealed envelope with the results in it. The entire gymnasium burst into applause as Quinn and Finn, who were strategically standing near the stage, headed up the steps and approached the microphone. The football players made *whoop-whoop* noises and pumped their fists enthusiastically in the air. Principal Figgins appeared onstage holding a plastic rhinestone tiara and crown.

Quinn felt like everything was moving in slow motion. All evening, people had been telling her they'd voted for her and Finn, so she wasn't totally surprised to hear Brittany announce her name. But she was surprised at how good it felt to walk up onstage to thundering applause, with everyone staring at her and all the girls wishing they could be her. She'd never felt such unadulterated power before, and she felt slightly dizzy with the realization that she was the most important girl at McKinley High. And Finn, her tall and handsome, if slightly blockheaded, date, was at her side.

It was more than she had dreamed of. It was absolutely perfect.

'Congratulations.' As she leaned forward slightly to enable Principal Figgins to place the tiara on her head and heard the snap of cell phone cameras taking her picture, she felt a smile – the first real smile of the night – slowly spreading across her face.

'Lean over, please,' Figgins instructed Finn, who towered over the principal. Finn awkwardly bent his knees and let Figgins place the crown on his head. Quinn, beaming at the crowd, felt her eyes linger on someone who had appeared near the center of the room.

It was Puck. His eyes locked with hers across the room. In his black suit and black dress shirt, no tie, he looked handsome in a rakish, dangerous way. Quinn still felt her knees wobble slightly as she thought of what had happened the other night, but something besides sexual tension passed between their eyes. As Santana clung to Puck's arm and Finn put his hand on Quinn's waist, an unspoken understanding passed between them.

This is how it should be. This is what she had always

wanted. What she wanted now. To be onstage with her male counterpart, poised to reign over the school. She was the good girl. She was the homecoming queen, and now she had to act the part.

And there was no room for Puck.

As she pressed her cheek to Finn's, she knew this was for the best. Puck was just a little temporary insanity – perhaps something with the moon cycles – but now she was back where she belonged. She breathed a sigh of relief.

Once the royalty had been crowned, the DJ started spinning music again. After a slow dance to celebrate the coronation, the music switched to faster tunes that everyone could dance to. The party started pumping.

'Is it time yet?' Mercedes asked, smoothing her skirt. 'I'm ready to kick it.'

Kurt rolled his eyes. He was still watching Finn and Quinn awkwardly attempt to dance while talking to the gaggle of people who had rushed up to congratulate them. 'Please. Let's do it soon. I can't take much more of the popular kids kissing each other's asses.'

'It's now or never,' Artie agreed.

'Wish me luck!' Rachel said brightly as she strode over to the DJ table. The DJ was a skinny guy in his mid-twenties with a goatee and greasy hair pulled into a ponytail. A ponytail? Really? Weren't those just for girls again? When Rachel got to the booth, she leaned forward and smiled at the DJ. 'You're doing a really super job tonight.'

The DJ blinked, as if he wasn't used to having girls talk to him. 'You think?' He leaned forward to hear Rachel over the music.

'Definitely.' Rachel blinked her eyelashes seductively at him. She was not a fan of heavy makeup, but she was grateful she'd applied an extra coat of mascara. The DJ seemed mesmerized by her eyes. 'What's your name?' She stared at the mole on his cheek so that her eyes wouldn't look at Kurt and Tina, who had sneaked behind him. They peered into a couple of boxes before pulling out five wireless microphones.

'Ricky,' he said, coughing into his hand. His skin was unnaturally pale, as if he'd spent his life underground. 'Can I…do you want me to play a song for you?'

'Yes,' Rachel answered, smiling.

Two minutes later, the first notes of Lady Gaga's 'Just Dance' pulsed through the sound system, and the kids went wild. Even people who had been lingering along the sidelines stepped out onto the floor and started to move to the music. Everyone except Kurt, who was crouched behind the DJ booth. The other Glee kids had slowly moved to the floor in front of the stage, each holding a microphone at his or her side. Finally, just when the song started to really heat up, Kurt plucked the plug from the receiver and scooted out onto the dance floor before Ricky could see what happened.

The music jerked to a stop. 'What the hell?' someone cried, and other kids booed and jeered until they started to hear something. A quiet gradually fell over the room. Someone was singing.

The Glee kids sang, picking up exactly where the song had left off. People standing near the front of the gym stepped back to give room to the kids with microphones, and people at the back of the crowd pushed forward to see who was singing. After a few moments of awe, all the kids in the room started tapping their feet and dancing, as if the change were intentional. A couple of them cheered.

Rachel's face burned with excitement as she sang, feeding on the stares of the crowd. They sounded incredible, she could tell already. Maybe it was the song, or maybe they just needed to be relaxed.

Or maybe they'd realized they could lose what they had in Glee if they didn't sing their hearts out.

Ricky the DJ quickly brought in an awesome beat to back them up, and even the chaperones found themselves tapping their feet to the music. Mr Schuester, who had been enduring an excruciating conversation with Ken Tanaka about athlete's foot, was blown away. Who were these kids? Not only were they talented but they were bold, shaking up the staid old homecoming dance with their little impromptu concert.

'These kids have a lot of potential,' Mr Schuester said to Ken.

'I guess.' The coach tugged at his belt. His dress shorts were a little too tight, and he felt uncomfortable in a room full of kids who weren't wearing gym clothes.

Mr Schuester wasn't the only person who was impressed. When the Glee kids had started singing, the group surrounding Quinn and Finn had rushed to see what was going on, leaving the two of them alone at the center of the room. Quinn had dragged him forward to see the action, edging her way past people until she was at the front of the crowd.

Quinn glanced at Finn, who seemed completely entranced by the performance. She followed his gaze to the figure of Rachel Berry, who was waltzing across the floor as if she owned it. Where the hell did they even get microphones from?

'This is not part of the scheduled programming,' Quinn spat out, annoyed. Tonight was supposed to be her night, and now Rachel Berry and her loser friends were spinning things out of control.

Finn could barely hear Quinn over the music and the foot-thumping from the crowd. 'They're pretty good, right?' He was thinking mostly of Rachel, though, who was going back and forth with the microphone like a real performer. She sounded better than Lady Gaga, and she didn't look nervous at all. She just looked like she was having a really great time.

Quinn's eyes narrowed. 'If you like that kind of thing,' she said. Which she didn't. She really didn't.

Her words were drowned out by the explosion of applause.

twenty-five

Principal Figgins's office, Monday morning

On Monday morning, the Glee kids were called out of homeroom into Mr Figgins's office. The weekend had been the exact opposite of the previous weekend, after their humiliating performance at the recital. Now, instead of being humiliated, they were completely elated, and the other Glee members had felt a burst of generosity toward Rachel. Even when she was quick to claim credit for the idea and their shot at redemption, they couldn't really hate her for bragging, even though it drove Mercedes crazy to admit it.

Tina, Kurt, Mercedes, and Rachel all crowded around Principal Figgins's desk. Artie couldn't fit past the armchairs and had to sit right inside the doorway. Coach Sylvester, in a royal-blue-and-yellow tracksuit, was standing off to the side, leaning against a radiator.

Rachel cleared her throat. Why was Coach Sylvester here, anyway? She didn't see why the Glee kids should be in any sort of trouble, but she was confident she could lead Glee out of it. In fact, she was confident about everything today. The homecoming dance could not have been more of a success, and all kinds of students had come up to the Glee kids after they had finished singing to tell them how awesome they were. Even though the Cheerios and football players pretended nothing had happened, Rachel could tell they were furious.

Which just made it all that much sweeter.

'I've called you here to talk about what happened at the homecoming dance on Friday,' Principal Figgins announced in his typical weary-sounding voice. He glanced at Coach Sylvester. 'Some people have, ahem, taken offense at your performance.'

'But we sounded magical,' Kurt said. The last time he had been called to Principal Figgins's office was after he'd been tied to the top of the goalpost during an outdoor gym class. He'd been unable to identify the perpetrators, since he'd kept his eyes closed the whole time.

'If what you mean by *magical* is disrespectful, atrocious, horrifying, then, yes, you sounded magical.' Two tiny beads of spittle clung to the corners of Coach Sylvester's mouth.

Principal Figgins held up a hand to silence Coach Sylvester.

'In cases of disturbance like this, I just like to call in the students themselves and ask them to explain what happened.'

'I'll tell you what happened.' Coach Sylvester sneered. 'These little Mouseketeers interrupted one of the most important rituals of a girl's high school career by jumping out on the floor in the middle of the homecoming dance and pulling a stunt like that. Acting like transvestites? Disgraceful.' She shook her head in disgust. 'I don't know how poor Quinn Fabray cried herself to sleep after you so brutally destroyed her night.'

'Principal Figgins, we didn't do our performance until after the king and queen's special dance was over, I swear.' Rachel tried not to look at Coach Sylvester, who she suspected would not be afraid to punch her if they ever happened to walk down an empty hallway together.

'That sort of excuse didn't work for the Nazis.' Coach Sylvester looked at Principal Figgins for support, but he just indicated to Rachel that she should keep explaining. He wished he were out golfing.

'Look, we only did it because we were virtually forced to. Glee Club has practically no opportunities to perform, because there's no money in the school budget for us. And Mr Ryerson's never around to help.' Rachel tucked her hair behind her ears. Tina gave her a small smile to keep her motivated. She felt good representing the other Glee kids to Principal Figgins, especially as she knew the two of them had a special relationship.

'But you performed at the Fall in Love with Music recital.' Principal Figgins stared out the window at the giant lawn mower that was speeding back and forth over the front lawn. He wondered who was behind the wheel. Probably that horrible Hank guy the city had sent over.

'Yes, but we were sabotaged by the Cheerios, who gave us a faulty fog machine that they had already tried to use and knew was dysfunctional.' Rachel's voice became even more passionate as she spoke about the ways she'd been wronged.

Principal Figgins blinked. 'Is that true, Sue? Were the Cheerios responsible for the fog machine? I had three parents go to the school nurse's office for smoke inhalation!'

'I doubt my girls had anything to do with that.' Coach Sylvester sniffed. 'They've been far too concerned with perfecting their routines for cheer regionals to have time to bother with immature high jinks with these Glee kids.'

'Speaking of high jinks, Coach Sylvester,' Rachel began, feeling her chest well up with the anticipation of triumph, 'I happened to overhear you telling Mrs Iggulden that you personally made sure that your head Cheerio, Quinn Fabray, and her boyfriend won the election by "buying" two hundred votes.'

'You can't vote in the homecoming election, Sue. You're not even a student here!' Principal Figgins was never surprised at Coach Sylvester's actions, though this time she seemed to have crossed the line. She was always pulling stunts like this. It was only because the Cheerios had won so many championships that he even put up with her. 'Explain yourself.'

Kurt nudged Mercedes in the ribs. This was delicious.

Coach Sylvester's face froze. She was not used to being challenged, not even by Figgins, and especially not in front of a group of singing losers. 'In order to maintain the moral structure that teenagers need—'

Principal Figgins cut her off. 'In order to maintain the moral structure that teenagers need, we as administrators need to set a good example.' The last thing he wanted to do, however, was have another homecoming election because one of his staff had corrupted this one. That would be too much of a headache. 'As a compromise to this problem, I suggest that the homecoming results stand. From what I've heard, Sue, your contribution was not even necessary. Everyone loves Quinn and Finn.' He shrugged. Finn Hudson was a nice boy, and Quinn Fabray seemed like a model student, except for her insistence that he let her start the Celibacy Club. 'And all the funds the Cheerios raised from the voting booth will go directly to Glee Club.'

'This will not stand.' Coach Sylvester's face went ashen. 'Those funds are to be funneled directly to the Cheerios' tanning fund. You have got to be kidding me.'

'I'm not kidding, Sue.' Principal Figgins stood up. He was ready for them all to leave his office.

Coach Sylvester's eyes looked like they were about to pop out of their sockets, but she made a relatively graceful exit.

'Okay, but I'm going to the parents about this. We can't win state with a bunch of albinos.' She gave Rachel a demonic glare, as if to say she wasn't done with her yet. Without another word, the coach disappeared into the hallway, kicking the secretary's garbage can for good measure on the way out.

The Glee kids beamed. It was almost too good to be true. 'Thank you, Principal Figgins, for your true understanding of fairness.' Rachel loved the smell of victory in the air.

Principal Figgins spoke up before Rachel Berry could keep babbling. 'Yes, yes. But no more unplugging expensive sound equipment. I don't need another lawsuit on my hands.'

The rest of them thanked Principal Figgins and left the office quickly, not wanting to give him time to change his mind.

'I can't believe it,' Tina whispered as they tiptoed away from the office. 'Did that really just happen? We're going to get some funding?'

'It's a start, at least,' Rachel declared. She was envisioning piles of sheet music, elaborate costumes, and state-of-the-art sound equipment. Or maybe what they really needed first was a faculty adviser, someone who could guide them to become better singers and performers. Or maybe they needed T-shirts!

'You were really cool in there, Rachel,' Artie said, adjusting his tie. 'The way you stood up to Figgins and Coach Sylvester like that.' He could see how her persistence would, in situations like these, come in handy.

'I suggest we all celebrate our latest victory with virgin mimosas.' Kurt clapped his hands together. 'Who's in?'

Everyone agreed except Rachel, who had glanced down the hall to see Finn Hudson hovering near the water fountain, pretending to take a drink of water. She could see the spray of water missing his mouth by several inches. Was he ... waiting to talk to her? 'I'll be there in a minute,' Rachel said, smoothing her pleated gray skirt. 'I've got to get something from my locker.'

As soon as the Glee kids walked away, Finn stood up and wiped his mouth. He glanced around him to see if any of his football buddies were in sight, and then he felt a stab of guilt. Why did he care who they saw him talking to? It was so stupid. He could do whatever he wanted. He was homecoming king, after all.

With that, he walked over to Rachel, who was fumbling through her backpack, pretending to look for something.

'Hey, Rachel.' Finn's tongue felt fat in his mouth, like the time he'd knocked down a bees' nest with a baseball bat and they'd all swarmed him. He got kind of nervous talking to Rachel – she just seemed so smart, if a little insane.

'Hi, Finn.' Rachel straightened up and smiled at him. She thought he was sort of like a hermit crab, reluctant to leave his shell. He just needed some coaxing from her. 'Congratulations on winning the coveted position of homecoming king.'

'Oh, yeah. Thanks.' Finn shook his head. It seemed silly for her to be congratulating him when all he'd done was walk up onstage and let Figgins put a crown on his head, which had been kind of awkward. Rachel was the one who'd managed to put on an awesome spontaneous performance at the dance with her geeky but talented friends, and the whole school had loved it. It would be nice to do something creative like that. Quinn, meanwhile, had fumed the whole way home and wouldn't even consider the hot-tub idea after that. 'I just heard this kind of rumor about you?'

'That's not true,' Rachel replied hotly. 'I have never dated something with four legs.'

'No, not that one.' Finn ran his hand across his head. 'That you were, maybe, transferring to some fancy arts school?'

'Oh.' Rachel had almost forgotten all about that idea. She was surprised the rumor mill had been spreading it – usually, if the news wasn't something nasty, no one cared. 'It's something I've been looking into.'

Maybe it was partly the Glee Club's recent success that made her think twice about transferring, but even before that, her heart just hadn't been in it. Maybe there were better schools for her to develop her talent, but McKinley High had one thing none of them did: Finn Hudson. She knew it was silly to base her decision – and possibly her entire future – on a boy she'd talked to a handful of times, but she couldn't help it. She knew something was there.

Finn nodded and leaned back against the lockers. He looked so casual and handsome, like a boy in the JCPenney ads that came in the mail. 'Well, I just wanted to tell you that I thought what you guys did at the dance was pretty cool. You sounded really good. And looked good.' He turned red. 'I mean, all of you. Not just you.'

Rachel's eyes widened. 'Thank you,' she said, her brain reeling. Finn really seemed nervous talking to her.

Finn shrugged. 'I just wanted to make sure I said something to you before you left.'

Rachel smiled sweetly. 'I've actually decided not to go anywhere. A certain person helped me change my mind about McKinley,' she added pointedly.

'Oh, cool.' Finn didn't seem to catch her reference, which was fine. He was dating Quinn Fabray, after all, and Rachel wasn't going to throw herself at him. Well, not exactly. But there was nothing wrong with letting him know what he was missing, was there? 'Their loss is McKinley's gain, then.'

Besides, Rachel thought, the performance at the dance – which had been almost completely spontaneous – had reminded her how easy it was to shine brighter when surrounded by mediocrity. She was ready to be the big fish – the biggest, glitteriest, most talented fish – in the very small pond of McKinley High. In fact, she was born ready for it.

'That's really nice of you to say.' Rachel glanced toward the cafeteria, and she saw the Glee kids waiting outside the door for her. 'I guess I'll see you around, Shark Finn,' she said sassily before she spun around on her heel and walked slowly away.

Finn stared after her, watching her cute butt sashay down the hallway. How did she know it had been him? 'Hey, wait a second!' His long legs only needed a couple of strides to catch up with her. He lowered his voice so no one nearby could hear. 'If you got my warning about the Cheerios messing up the recital, why did you still go on?'

'No offense, since I know you're dating one, but the Cheerios don't rule the world, and I'm not going to let them tell me what I can and can't do.' Rachel's lips tingled from being so close to Finn. She'd had a dream the other night in which they were sitting in a library – a nice one, with leather books and chairs, not like the school library – and he looked up from a book and leaned over to kiss her. When she woke up, her body tingled all over. The kiss had felt real – so real she felt like the dream was a premonition. She was going to kiss Finn Hudson someday.

'That's probably a good policy.' Finn gave her a half wave and turned away. He had a funny feeling in his stomach, like he'd eaten too much shrimp or something.

Rachel grinned to herself as she walked away. Up ahead, she could see a football player take Kurt's math book and throw it in the trash. Okay, so maybe things weren't completely different yet, but at least they were heading in the right direction. Glee Club had entertained the entire school at the dance, and Finn Hudson was talking to her. Someday, she might even kiss him.

'Good morning, ladies and gentlemen of McKinley High,' Rachel said into the announcement-room microphone a few minutes later. When Principal Figgins had originally agreed to let Rachel run the morning announcements on a two-week trial basis, he probably had no idea how excellent she was going to be. He was most likely going to be heartbroken that this would be her final broadcast – it wasn't *that* inconceivable that her cheerful morning updates were like a ray of sunshine in his otherwise depressing day.

'As you all know, this weekend saw our very own McKinley High football team lead a valiant effort against Central Valley. While we did not win the game, I know everyone – myself included – is proud of our team.' Rachel paused. She wondered whether Finn knew she meant him. She wasn't really proud of anyone else.

She took a deep breath so the next words wouldn't get stuck in her throat. 'Also, I'd like to extend my congratulations to the new homecoming king and queen, Finn Hudson and Quinn Fabray.' But, really, she wasn't jealous. She never wanted to be someone who was admired just for her outer beauty, like Quinn. It might be nice for a while, but Rachel would much prefer that people admire her for her amazing talents instead.

Besides, if Quinn's boyfriend kept having 'moments' with Rachel, Quinn's life couldn't be *that* perfect.

'But most of all,' Rachel's voice boomed through the classrooms, 'thank you, everyone, for your undivided support of the brief Glee performance at the dance. You'll all be happy to know that Glee Club has, at long last, been awarded substantial funding, and you will definitely see more of us in the future.' She didn't care if Coach Sylvester came bursting into the room threatening to suffocate her with a pair of red-and-white pom-poms; Rachel had earned the right to give herself a little pat on the back. And the other Glee kids, too, of course.

'In the meantime, I'll leave you with some words from Tom Petty.' Tom Petty wasn't her favorite recording artist, but she couldn't find a more perfect song than 'I Won't Back Down'. She belted out the lyrics with power. Rachel backed away from the microphone, unable to keep the grin off her face. She imagined the lyrics slowly sinking into the conscious brains of the McKinley High students and faculty, courtesy of her own sweet voice.

The year was off to a pretty great start, after all.

As Rachel strolled away from the announcements office, Mr Schuester approached Mr Figgins's office from the opposite end of the hall.

'Figgins? I wanted to talk to you about the Glee Club.'

Can Rachel Berry rock a beret?

GLEETASTIC POSTER INSIDE!

glee

FOREIGN EXCHANGE

AN ORIGINAL NOVEL

BASED ON THE SERIES CREATED BY RYAN MURPHY & BRAD FALCHUK & IAN BRENNAN

February 2011

McKinley High goes international when a French glee
club comes to town in the second original Glee novel.

www.gleebooks.co.uk

BOB307

"Sloppy freak show babies!"

SEASON 1 VOLUME 2 AND THE COMPLETE FIRST SEASON ON DVD SEPTEMBER 1